HANG TILL DEATH

HANG TILL DEATH

India's Most Notorious Cases of Capital Punishment

Prateek Jain

BLOOMSBURY

NEW DELHI • LONDON • OXFORD • NEW YORK • SYDNEY

BLOOMSBURY INDIA
Bloomsbury Publishing India Pvt. Ltd
Second Floor, LSC Building No. 4, DDA Complex, Pocket C – 6 & 7,
Vasant Kunj, New Delhi 110070

BLOOMSBURY, BLOOMSBURY PRIME and the Diana logo are trademarks of Bloomsbury Publishing Plc

First published 2020

ISBN: 978-93-87457-53-9

2 4 6 8 10 9 7 5 3 1

Printed and bound in India by Thomson Press India Ltd.

The infectiousness of crime is like that of the plague.

—Napoleon Bonaparte

Contents

Contents

Preface

Many things happen around us. While TV channels and newspapers bring a lot of these stories to light, there are many more which are lost to us. And then, there are stories which we have heard about but find it hard to tell. These are the stories that give us nightmares and make us anxious, but still we try to live with courage and hope.

During these rapidly changing times, with crimes occurring at unprecedented levels, security has become a primary concern. A crime occurs every time safety and security is violated; a sin is committed and a culprit is born. Each crime has a story behind it. This book brings to light 11 such famous stories of revenge, inhumanity, flesh and blood.

According to a report published by the National Crime Records Bureau (NCRB) in 2016, crimes rates in India are as follows:

An Executive Summary of Crime in India—2016 (States/UTs)

Crime Head	Crime Incidence			Crime Rate			Percentage Variation	
	2014	2015	2016	2014	2015	2016	2014 - 2015	2015 - 2016
IPC	2,851,563	2,949,400	2,975,711	229.2	234.2	233.6	3.4%	0.9%
SLL	1,720,100	1,761,276	1,855,804	138.3	139.9	145.7	2.4%	5.4%
Total	4,571,663	4,710,676	4,831,515	367.5	374.1	379.3	3.0%	2.6%

Source: Data from National Crime Records Bureau. 2016. 'Crime in India—2016' Government of India, xvii.

i. A total of 4,831,515 cognisable crimes comprising 2,975,711 Indian Penal Code (IPC) crimes and 1,855,804 Special & Local Laws (SLL) crimes were reported in 2016, showing an increase of 2.6% over 2015 (4,710,676 cases).
ii. During 2016, IPC crimes have increased by 0.9% and SLL crimes have increased by 5.4% over 2015.
iii. Percentage share of IPC was 61.6% while percentage share of SLL cases was 38.4% of total cognizable crimes during 2016.
iv. Uttar Pradesh accounted for 9.5% of total IPC crime reported in the country followed by Madhya Pradesh (8.9%), Maharashtra (8.8%) and Kerala (8.7%).
v. Delhi reported the highest crime rate (974.9) under IPC crimes followed by Kerala (727.6) against national average of 233.6.
vi. Kerala has reported highest number of cases of SLL crimes (24.1%) followed by Gujarat and Tamil Nadu (15.5% each) of total SLL crimes reported in the country during 2016.
vii. Kerala reported highest SLL crime rate of 1,252.7 in the country during 2016 followed by Gujarat (457.1) against national average of 145.7.

IPC Crimes 2014–2016

S. No.	Crime Head	2014		2015			2016	
		Incidence	Crime Rate	Incidence	Crime Rate	Inci-dence	Crime Rate	Percentage Share to IPC Crimes
1	2	3	4	5	6	7	8	9
A. Offences Affecting the Human Body								
1	Murder	33,981	2.7	32,127	2.6	30,450	2.4	1.0
2	Culpable Homicide not Amounting to Murder	3,332	0.3	3,176	0.3	3,203	0.3	0.1
3	Causing Death by Negligence	128,771	10.4	134,384	10.7	140,215	11.0	4.7
4	Dowry Deaths $	8,455	1.4	7,634	1.3	7,621	1.2	0.3
5	Attempt to Commit Murder	41,791	3.4	46,471	3.7	49,667	3.9	1.7
6	Attempt to Commit Culpable Homicide	4,358	0.4	6,118	0.5	7,527	0.6	0.3
7	Grievous Hurt	105,201	8.5	92,996	7.4	89,039	7.0	3.0

S. No.	Crime Head	2014		2015		2016		
		Incidence	Crime Rate	Incidence	Crime Rate	Inci-dence	Crime Rate	Percentage Share to IPC Crimes
1	2	3	4	5	6	7	8	9
8	Causing Simple & Grievous Injuries under Rash Driving	409,899	32.9	451,069	35.8	348,914	27.4	11.7
9	Assault on Women with Intent to Outrage her Modesty $	82,235	13.7	82,422	13.6	84,746	13.8	2.8
10	Kidnapping & Abduction	77,237	6.2	82,999	6.6	88,008	6.9	3.0
11	Human Trafficking	733	0.1	1,027	0.2	918	0.1	0.0
12	Rape $	36,735	6.1	34,651	5.7	38,947	6.3	1.3
13	Attempt to Commit Rape $	4,234	0.7	4,437	0.7	5,729	0.9	0.2
14	Unnatural Offences	1,148	0.1	1,347	0.1	2,187	0.2	0.1
Total (A)		**938,110**	**75.4**	**980,858**	**77.9**	**897,171**	**70.4**	**30.1**

Source: Data from National Crime Records Bureau. 2016. 'Crime in India—2016' Government of India, 4.

The Republic of India, the world's seventh largest country by area and the most populous democracy, is battling increasing levels of crime. Among the many culprits who execute crimes, a considerable percentage find themselves behind bars as per the law. Among those who are imprisoned, some are set free upon completion of their sentence while others, according to their sentences, remain confined for the entire duration of their lives. And, apart from those convicts facing life imprisonment, there is a small number that receives the ultimate punishment, the death sentence.

> Murder rates have approximately doubled from 1973 (17,072) to 2016 (30,450). The murder rates continued to rise in the subsequent years. The maximum that it reached was in the year 1992 (40,105). The statistics gives us the clear picture of the society that we live in. Rape statistics have surpassed all the boundaries in India. 2,919 rapes were recorded in the year 1973, in the year 2016 the recorded number is 38,947. The record shows that the rape rates have increased 13 times. The statistics have recorded every year a higher number than the previous year. This clear shows that rape laws have increased despite of all the laws.
>
> Kidnapping too, like rape and murder, has shown an upward trend. 1973 recorded total of 10,223 and 2016 recorded a total of 88,008.

> The rates of kidnapping have gone up 8 times in 43 years. This again shows the failure of law as a mechanism to civilize people. Therefore, the statistics proves that crime against human body has increased significantly in the last 43 years.[1]

After the nation achieved independence in 1947, the first death sentence was carried out on 15 November 1949, when Nathuram Godse and Narayan Apte were hung to death for the assassination of Mahatma Gandhi. Yakub Abdul Razak Memon, who was convicted over his involvement in the 1993 Bombay bombings, was executed by hanging on 30 July 2015 in Nagpur jail. It was the last time a death sentence was executed in India. This book retells 11 high-profile cases which ended with a death sentence; in each instance documenting the convict's initial life, their entry into a deviant life of vengeance and brutalism, the details of the crimes they were convicted for and finally their last days before the execution. Justice may be delayed, but it will never be denied, irrespective of what obstacles lie in the path. These 11 stories prove this fact.

How much do we know of these incidents that shook our country? What was the origin and motivation behind these crimes? And how did their lives come to an end? How much do we know of the legal system of India?

---

1 http://ncrb.gov.in/StatPublications/CII/CII2016/pdfs/Crime%20Statistics%20-%202016.pdf

This book makes an honest attempt to answer these questions. The particulars of each case are based on reports that surfaced when the incidents happened—various newspaper, magazine and internet articles, and e-media reports and interviews. Each case has been narrated chronologically and written succinctly in the hopes of making it an easy and interesting read.

Introduction: Living with the Rules

Criminal law enforces and regulates social conduct, in addition to prohibiting threats or any elements that might endanger the health, safety and moral welfare of the people under its jurisdiction. Criminal law also enforces punishment of offenders who violate the law.

Punishment is the infliction of an unpleasant or negative experience on an offender in response to an offense. In ancient times, the sole purpose of punishment was retribution. However, in more modern societies the objectives of punishment include deterrence, retribution, incapacitation, rehabilitation, prevention and reparation. In order for a punishment to be justified, it must satisfy at least one of these criteria. But there may be reasons to oppose a punishment even when it does satisfy these criteria. In such cases, these can be considered as necessary but not sufficient conditions.

DETERRENCE

The theory of deterrence holds that the object of punishment is not only to prevent the wrongdoer from doing a wrong for the second time but also to set an example for others who may exhibit criminal tendencies. Deterrence can be divided into two types—general and specific. General deterrence is the use of punishment to discourage others who may be inclined to committing any such offense. Specific deterrence is used to prevent the offender from committing any further offense.

However, this theory has been criticised on the grounds that it has proved ineffective in reducing crime, and that excessive punishment tends to defeat its own purpose by arousing the sympathy of the public towards those who receive cruel and inhuman punishment.

RETRIBUTION

In primitive societies, punishment primarily served a retributive function that aimed at making the offenders suffer for their crimes. The wronged person was granted the opportunity to exact revenge against the wrongdoer. The idea of retribution as an objective of punishment is encapsulated in the saying: 'an eye for an eye'.

Many would argue that a criminal deserves to suffer. Retributive punishment gratifies the instinct for revenge or retaliation, which exists not only in the individual wronged but also in society at large. In modern times, the state has come forward to effect revenge in place of the private individual. However, critics of the retributive theory of punishment point out that punishment per se is not a remedy for the mischief the offender has committed.

INCARCERATION AND REHABILITATION

Incarceration as an objective of punishment seeks to remove the offender from society for the good of society. It can be justified by three actionable goals:

1. incapacitation,
2. specific deterrence and
3. general deterrence.

Incarceration incapacitates by preventing inmates from committing new crimes outside prison. Incarceration can serve as a specific deterrent insofar as individuals who have served time behind bars are less inclined to commit new crimes after their release. Incarceration can serve as a general deterrent, as individuals who have not been incarcerated are less inclined to commit crimes because of the fear of incarceration. All three goals can be in service of public safety.

REPARATION

Reparation means that the offender must compensate the victim as part of the punishment and as a condition for their re-entry into society. Reparation constitutes restorative justice, in other words, 'rebalancing the scales' when a wrong has been committed. For instance, vandals being ordered to clean up graffiti or arsonists rebuilding the structures they have damaged. A reparation order can be of two kinds:

> A compensation order—where an offender makes a compensation payment to the victim of the crime.

A restitution order—requiring that property is returned to the victim.

A reparation order is on top of, and not part of, the sentence imposed on an offender. It may be made by a court on its own initiative or following an application from a victim or the prosecutor.

A court cannot make a compensation order if it is believed that: the offender could not comply with the order due to insufficient means and paying the compensation would unduly prejudice the welfare of the offender's dependants.[1]

PREVENTION

The criminal justice system prevents offenders from repeating their crimes by awarding punishments, such as death, exile or forfeiture of an office. By putting the criminal in jail, the individual is prevented from committing other crimes. Rule 58 of the International Standard Minimum Rules states that:

> The purpose and justification of a sentence of imprisonment or a similar measure derivative of liberty is ultimately to protect society against crime. This end can only be achieved if the period of imprisonment is used to ensure, so far as possible, that upon his return to society, the

1 Department of Justice. 2017. 'Restitution and Reparation'. Available at: https://courts.justice.wa.gov.au/R/restitution_reparation.aspx?-uid=8336-5958-9621-6137 (accessed on 25 April 2019).

offender is not only willing, but also able to lead a law-abiding and self-supporting life.[2]

MULTIPLE APPROACH THEORY

Punishment should be in proportion to the nature and gravity of the crime. Under certain conditions, a criminal should be able to secure his release by demonstrating improvement in his conduct. A perfect system of criminal justice could never be based on any single theory of justice. Instead, it requires a combination of them all, hence, we have the multiple approach theory.

Each individual, and indeed each society, has its own views on how and why we punish criminals. Most people want to stop crime from happening, but they believe this goal is best achieved through different means.

Christianity teaches that sin is an integral part of human nature, and every human being has the potential to commit a crime. This is shown in the story of the fall of Adam and Eve in the book of Genesis in the Bible when they disobeyed God and ate the forbidden fruit.

Many Christians believe that the Bible teaches the difference between right and wrong. Following God's will leads people to the right path, and ignoring God's will leads to disasters.

Hindus believe that in order to achieve higher spiritual goals, they must follow the path of dharma. This concept of justice is linked to the principles of karma and ahimsa. The actions of an individual in one

---

[2] Available at: https://www.unodc.org/pdf/criminal_justice/UN_Standard_Minimum_Rules_for_the_Treatment_of_Prisoners.pdf.

life will directly affect his/her experiences in future existences. Bad or negative actions will lead to karmic debt. Some Hindus would say that people have many 'lessons to learn' in terms of karma, and they need to be reborn many times in order to attain moksha.

Muslims believe in the sanctity of life and, therefore, they do not think anybody has the right to disrespect human life. Justice is an important teaching in Islam. Islamic law sets out how Muslims should behave in order to live the life that Allah intends them to live; that is to be in harmony with others and their environment. If a person breaks a law, it is seen as going against the principles and rules set by the Quran and Sunnah. Some countries have legal systems based on the Shariah Law, such as Saudi Arabia and Iran. Most Muslims believe that if a person commits a crime they should be punished by law, but they will also have to answer to Allah on the Day of Judgement.

Sikhs believe that according to the law of karma, unjust people and criminals will be judged and punished by God. God will ensure that everyone receives justice at the end of their lives. Sikhs will also follow the lives of the Gurus and the teaching laid out in the Guru Granth Sahib.

Individual and religious beliefs may affect one's conception of the aims of punishment and accordingly its most effective form.

WHAT IS CAPITAL PUNISHMENT?

Capital punishment is the execution of any individual who has been found guilty of certain exceptional crimes.

The term stems from the Latin word *capitalis*, meaning 'regarding the head', and originally referred to beheading.

Capital punishment is prevalent in quite a few countries around the world, though the number is dwindling now. According to Amnesty International[3], as of 2017, 142 countries have abolished the death penalty either in law on in practice, and that in the past five years 33 countries have carried out at least one execution. Four countries were responsible for 84 per cent of the executions in 2017 (Saudi Arabia, Iraq, Pakistan and Iran). China is not included in the list as the statistics of capital punishment is a state secret. Amnesty estimates that China carries out thousands of executions each year.[4] In many countries, death sentences are not carried out immediately after being handed down; there is often a long period of uncertainty for the convicted while their cases are appealed to in higher courts.

The countries that carried out executions between 2013 and 2017 are Afghanistan, Bahrain, Bangladesh, Belarus, Botswana, Chad, China, Egypt, Equatorial Guinea, India, Indonesia, Iran, Iraq, Japan, Jordan, Kuwait, Malaysia, Nigeria, North Korea, Oman, Pakistan, Palestinian Territories, Saudi Arabia, Singapore, Somalia, South Sudan, Sudan, Taiwan, Thailand, United Arab Emirates, USA, Vietnam and Yemen. Due to ongoing conflicts in Libya and Syria,

---

[3] See https://www.amnesty.org/en/.

[4] *BBC News*. 2018. 'Death penalty: How many countries still have it?' *BBC News*, London, 14 October.

Amnesty International was not able to confirm whether judicial executions were carried out in these countries. The 21 countries that did not carry out an execution in those years despite not having abolished death penalty are Antigua and Barbuda, Bahamas, Barbados, Belize, Comoros, Cuba, Democratic Republic of the Congo, Dominica, Ethiopia, Gambia, Guyana, Jamaica, Lebanon, Lesotho, Qatar, Saint Kitts and Nevis, Saint Lucia, Saint Vincent and the Grenadines, Trinidad and Tobago, Uganda and Zimbabwe.[5]

How do we define capital punishment? Capital punishment is frequently used interchangeably with the death penalty. Death penalty refers to the penalty received and not necessarily its implementation, whereas capital punishment refers to the execution itself. So to put it concisely, capital punishment is the practice of executing an individual as punishment for a specific crime following the conclusion of a legal trial. It is the most serious form of punishment the law can apply to a convicted person. Sentences of capital punishment are typically only attached to particularly egregious cases of murder. However, in Saudi Arabia, Iraq, Pakistan and Iran, treason, types of fraud, adultery and rape can also be considered capital crimes.

Types of Capital Punishment

Hanging

Execution by hanging is the most common method of capital punishment. Iran, where 369 people were

[5] Ibid.

reported to have been executed in 2013, has the highest number of cases of execution by hanging in the world. Other countries that carried out executions by hanging in 2013 are Afghanistan, Bangladesh, Botswana, India, Iraq, Japan, Kuwait, Malaysia, Nigeria, the Palestinian Authority in Gaza, South Sudan and Sudan.

Firing squad

Firing squad is the preferred method of execution in Indonesia. Twelve armed executioners shoot the prisoner in the chest. If the prisoner is still not dead, the commander then issues a final bullet to the head. Other countries that carry out executions by firing squad include China, North Korea, Saudi Arabia, Somalia, Taiwan and Yemen. It is also a preferred method of execution in the United Arab Emirates.

Beheadings

Saudi Arabia is the only country in the world where beheadings are used as a method of capital punishment. The beheadings are performed publicly with a sword.

Lethal injection

Lethal injection is often viewed as the least cruel method of execution. Injecting a fatal dose of drugs into a death-row inmate has become the primary method of execution in the United States. In 2013, lethal injection was also used in China and Vietnam.

Electrocution

The United States is the only country in the world to exercise capital punishment using electrocution in 2013. Previous electric chair executions sparked outrage. In 1997, convicted murderer Pedro Medina was executed by using an electric chair in Florida. His head burst into flames during the procedure. In 2008, the Nebraska Supreme Court declared execution by electrocution illegal for being a cruel and unusual punishment.

Origin

We can trace the origin of the term 'capital punishment' to ancient Greece. Capital punishment for murder, treason, arson and rape was widely employed in ancient Greece under the laws of Draco around 7th century BCE. Draco, also known as Drakon, was the first recorded legislator of Athens in Ancient Greece. He replaced the prevailing system of oral law and blood feud with a written code to be enforced only by a court of law. The ancient Romans also used capital punishment for a wide range of offenses. Most of the world's major religions have also sanctioned capital punishment at one time or another.

England also has a lengthy history of employing capital punishment. Death was formerly the penalty for a large number of offenses in England during the 17th and 18th centuries. Historically, executions were public events, attended by large crowds, and the mutilated bodies were often displayed while they were left to rot. Public executions were banned in England in 1868, although they continued to take place in parts of the US until the 1930s.

In India, the Indian Penal Code (IPC) is the law that states the punishable offences in India, along with their punishments or penalty or both. Alongside the IPC, the Criminal Procedure Code (CrPC) pertains to the law that describes the overall procedure which is to be followed while undertaking a criminal case. The IPC and the CrPC are two such laws which are created during the British Raj in India, which help the plaintiff to get justice.

In India

The history of capital punishment in modern India can be traced back to the year 1860 when the practice was incorporated into the IPC. It continued to remain in effect after independence in 1947. The first death sentence in independent India was executed on 15 November 1949, when Nathuram Godse and Narayan Apte were hanged to death for assassination the Father of the Nation, Mahatma Gandhi.

Article 21 of the Indian Constitution states that no person shall be deprived of his life and liberty except according to the procedure laid down by law. Under this article, every person has a right to life guaranteed by the Constitution. The IPC declares a death sentence for various offenses like criminal conspiracy, murder, waging war against the nation, dacoity (armed robbery or banditry), murder, etc. Various other legislation, such as the Narcotic Drugs and Psychotropic Substances Act, 1985, and Unlawful Activities Prevention Act, 1967, have provisions for the death penalty.

Article 72 of the Indian Constitution has created a provision for clemency whenever a death sentence is awarded. Under this article, the president has been given the power to grant pardons, reprieves, respites or remissions of punishment or to suspend, remit or commute the sentence of any person convicted of any offence.

Article 161 of the Indian Constitution provides similar powers to the governor of a state to grant clemency. When a Sessions Court awards capital punishment, it must be confirmed by the High Court of that state, and only then the execution can be carried out.

Provisions in the IPC

The IPC prescribes capital punishment for the following offences:

1. Murder (Section 302)
2. Abetment of suicide by a minor, insane person or intoxicated person (Section 305)
3. Threatening or inducing any person to give false evidence resulting in the conviction and death of an innocent person (Section 195-A)
4. Perjury, resulting in the conviction and death of an innocent person (Section 194)
5. Treason, for waging war against the Government of India (Section 121)
6. Abetment of mutiny actually committed (Section 132)
7. Attempted murder by a serving life convict (Section 307(2))
8. Kidnapping for ransom (Section 364-A)

9. Dacoity along with murder (Section 396)
10. Criminal conspiracy to commit any offence punishable with death, if committed in consequence thereof for which no punishment is prescribed (Section 120-B)
11. Joint liability extending the principle of constructive liability on all the persons who conjointly commit an offence punishable with death (Sections 34 and 49)
12. Abetment of offences punishable with death (Section 109)
13. Special and local laws:
    - Unlawful Activities Prevention Act, 1967 (as amended in 2004)
    - Defence and Internal Security of India Act, 1971
    - Defence of India Act, 1971
    - Commission of Sati (Prevention) Act, 1987
    - Narcotic Drugs and Psychotropic Substances (Prevention) Act, 1985 (as amended in 1988)
    - Terrorist and Disruptive Activities (Prevention) Act (TADA), 1987
    - Prevention of Terrorism Act (POTA), 2002
    - Scheduled Castes and Scheduled Tribes (Prevention of Atrocities) Act, 1989
    - Explosive Substances Act, 1908 (as amended in 2001)
    - Arms Act, 1959 (as amended in 1988)
    - Laws relating to the Armed Forces, for example, the Air Force Act, 1950; the Army Act, 1950; the Navy Act, 1950; and the Indo-Tibetan Border Police Force Act, 1992

- Various states (Andhra Pradesh, Karnataka, Arunachal Pradesh and Maharashtra) have control of Organised Crime Acts which entail the death penalty

14. Death penalty under defence laws:
    As a rule, the members of the forces of the Union of India are subject to the provisions of military laws, but in certain situations, an ordinary member of the public renders himself liable to be tried by court martial for the violation of the provisions of the defence laws. The general court martial constituted under the defence laws can pass a sentence of death on a person found guilty of Sections 34 and 37 of the Army Act. The abetment of the offences punishable with death, if committed in consequence of the abetment, is punishable with death under Section 66 of the Act.

The Execution

The execution of the death sentence in India calls for hanging by the neck till death according to the CrPC in 1973. CrPC Section 354-(5) mentions that if any person is sentenced to death, the sentence shall direct that the person be hanged by the neck till the person is dead.

Some Well-Known Cases in India

Jagmohan Singh vs State of Uttar Pradesh
Supreme Court, 3 October 1972
Jagmohan Singh had been convicted under IPC Section 302 for the murder of Chhotey Singh, and sentenced

to death by the Allahabad High Court. This was one of the first cases that challenged the death sentence awarded. Many arguments were put forward to contest the defendant's execution. First, the defence argued that the punishment deprived a person of the freedom of expression. Second, there were no legislative guidelines or standards laid down to determine who should live or die.

Around six or seven years before Chhotey Singh's murder, Jamohan Singh's uncle had been murdered. Chhotey Singh, who had been charged for that murder, was acquitted by the High Court. This was the reason for the animosity between the two.

A day before Chhotey Singh's murder, there had been an argument concerning irrigation of their fields between him and Jagmohan Singh. Shivraj Singh's son, Jagbir Singh had also been involved. Though the matter was resolved by the villagers who had gathered at the scene, it did not end there. The next day, on 10 September 1969, in the evening, Jagmohan and Jagbir, hid in the fields to catch Chhotey Singh off guard. Jagmohan had gotten hold of a country-made pistol, while Jagbir was armed with a lathi.

When Chhotey Singh realised that they were waiting for him, he decided to flee the scene. While chasing him, Jagmohan Singh fired at him and he succumbed to his injuries.

During the trial, though the death sentence awarded by the sessions judge was challenged, the judgment was confirmed as just and proper by the High Court and Jagmohan Singh was hanged.

Bachan Singh vs State of Punjab
9 May 1980
The appellant Bachan Singh was tried, convicted and sentenced by the sessions judge to death under Section 302 of the IPC for the murders of Desa Singh, Durga Bai and Veeran Bai, daughters of Hukam Singh, and causing grievous injuries to Vidya Bai, another daughter of Hukam Singh, at midnight between 4 and 5 July 1977, in the courtyard of the house of Hukam Singh. The judge found him guilty of the three charges under Section 302 IPC and sentenced him to death on each count. He also found him guilty under Section 326 IPC, for causing grievous hurt with a sharp weapon to Vidya Bai and sentenced him to three years of rigorous imprisonment and ordered him to pay a fine of Rs 500. Against the convictions and sentences passed, the appellant preferred Criminal Appeal 234 of 1978 to the High Court. The High Court dismissed his appeal and confirmed his death sentence. Appealing to the Supreme Court by special leave, a bench of the Supreme Court directed the records of the case to be submitted to the Chief Justice of India (CJI) to resolve the question of the constitutional validity of the death penalty for murder provided in Section 302. The Supreme court ruled that the death penalty should be imposed only in 'the rarest of rare cases' and honour killings fall within this category; the court thus recommended the death penalty be extended to those found committing honour killings.

Mithu Singh vs State of Punjab
7 April 1983
In India, capital punishment used to be mandatory under Section 303 IPC. It states that whoever, being under sentence of imprisonment for life, commits murder, shall be punished with death.

But the decision of the Supreme Court delivered on 7 April 1983 disposing of a writ petition filed by Mithu Singh and others challenging the constitutional validity of Section 303. Mithu Singh challenged it on the grounds that it violated Articles 14 and 21 of the Constitution, that 'no person deprived of his life on personal liberty except according to the procedure established by law'. The five Judges Constitution Bench presided over by Chief Justice Chinnappa Reddy, concurred that Section 303 IPC is unconstitutional and void. It violated the guarantee of equality contained in Article 14 as well as the right conferred by Article 21, which states that no person shall be deprived of his life or personal liberty except according to the procedure established by law. On these grounds, Section 303 which facilitated mandatory death penalty was scrapped and it was decided that thereafter, all murder cases, wherein a death sentence is awarded, will be tried under Section 302.

1

Nathuram Godse and Narayan Apte

Situated in Tees January Road, New Delhi, the sprawling Gandhi Smriti (formerly known as Birla House) has a quadrangular structure in the middle of a lush lawn. The Martyr's Column, built as a remembrance spot, marks the exact spot where the blood of the Father of the Nation was spilt when he was assassinated on 30 January 1948. This is the exact location where the country's most shocking conspiracy was executed, leaving behind an indelible mark on a newly independent India.

AN ASSASSIN'S HISTORY

Vinayak Vamanrao Godse, a postal employee in British India, and his wife Lakshmi lived in Baramati, Pune district, Bombay Presidency. They were Chitpavan Brahmins, renowned for their high-caste status. Vinayak had a government job that allowed him to support his family adequately; they led a simple life. However, fate was not kind to them. Lakshmi gave birth and lost three boys during their infancy consecutively, leaving the family mired with loss and despair. Finally, a daughter was born who was spared the fate of her brothers. Once it was clear that she would survive, the couple sighed in relief.

Although it took them a long time to recover from the loss of their sons, Vinayak and Lakshmi gradually started looking forward to their lives—their daughter became their source of happiness. On 19 May 1910, Lakshmi gave birth to another child. It was a boy this time, and he was named Ramachandra Vinayak Godse. However, old memories flooded back and Lakshmi was petrified that this son would die too; just like the nightmares of her previous pregnancies. She shared her fears with her husband. Was there was a curse on the male children of their family? Fearing that something ominous would again befall them, the couple decided that baby Ramachandra would be brought up as a girl for the first few years of his life. He was even made to wear a nose-ring, a *nath*, to dupe fate. Thus came about the moniker, Nathuram. When another boy was born, Nathuram's parents stopped treating him as a girl. But by this time, the moniker had stuck to him and remained with him for the rest of his life.

Nathuram studied in a local school in Baramati. Growing up, he heard a name often repeated around him wherever he went. The name was Mohandas Karamchand Gandhi, a skilled barrister who was battling the British imperial power with the philosophy of non-violence. He sometimes heard about Gandhi's adventures from his father. He was fascinated by

Gandhi and used to avidly follow his activities. Nathuram studied in that school till grade five. After that, he left the school because his parents wanted him to study in an English-medium school, which was necessary for a government job. He was sent to live with an aunt in Pune where his parents hoped he would fulfil their dreams.

The 1920s and 1930s were marked with the British Raj's oppression of its Indian subjects. Nationalism and the demand for dominion status were growing, and Indians were increasingly becoming aware of the exploitative laws and policies of the British. Mahatma Gandhi's request to abolish all the repressive laws written by the British was rejected by the then Viceroy of British India, Lord Irwin. He rejected all his eleven demands. When his demands were refused, Gandhi initiated the Civil Disobedience Movement, leading the Dandi March on 12 March 1930. He, along with 78 of his followers, marched from Sabarmati Ashram to Dandi, situated on the coast of Gujarat. They travelled a distance of 200 miles and violated the salt law by making salt from seawater. This was a symbolic move; with one simple action, Gandhi instigated the nation to break British law everywhere.

The movement caused widespread enthusiasm among the people and drew worldwide attention to the Indian independence movement. The British Parliament and media noted this, which made the British Prime Minister Ramsay MacDonald call for the First Round Table Conference in London. While the Indian National Congress (INC) and the most business leaders bycotted the First Round Table Conference, the Muslim league, the Hindu Mahasabha, the liberals and princes attended it. Many of the Congress leaders were put in jail for their involvement in the Civil Disobedience Movement.

After the Congress refused to join the conference, and no one could not get any fruitful result due to the absence of any Congress leaders, the government started to convince the Congress to participate in the Second Round Table conference in 1931. On January 1931, Gandhi and all other members were released unconditionally.

Finally Gandhi was convinced to negotiate with Viceroy Lord Irwin and they signed the Gandhi–Irwin Pact, which placed the Congress on an equal footing with the government.

On 5 March 1931, they agreed to pave way for Congress' participation in the Second Round Table Conference. The Congress would discontinue the Civil Disobedience Movement and participate in the Second Round Table Conference. The government would withdraw all ordinances issued to curb the Congress, withdraw all prosecutions relating to offenses not involving violence and release all persons undergoing sentences of imprisonment for their activities in the Civil Disobedience Movement.

The Second Round Table Conference was held in London from 7 September 1931 to 1 December 1931 with the participation of Gandhi and the Indian National Congress. Two weeks before the Conference was convened, the Labour government had been replaced by the Conservatives. At the conference, Gandhi claimed to represent the people of India. This view, however, was not shared by the other delegates. In fact, the division between the many attending groups was one of the reasons why the outcomes of the Second Round Table Conference were again of no substantial results regarding India's constitutional future. Meanwhile, civil unrest had spread throughout India again. Upon his return to India, Gandhi was arrested along with other Congress leaders. A separate province of Sind was created and the interests of minorities were safeguarded by MacDonald's Communal Award.

Nathuram Godse kept a close eye on the Civil Disobedience Movement. He respected Gandhi's defiance of the imperial laws and supported the popular movement but did not agree with his methods. This was also the time when he gravitated towards the freedom movement, aiming to contribute, and dropped out of school. He became a member of the Hindu nationalist organisation Rashtriya Swayamsevak Sangh (RSS)1.

Nathuram eventually left the RSS and joined the Hindu Mahasabha[2]. It was here that Nathuram met Veer Savarkar.

---

[1] Rashtriya Swayamsevak Sangh was founded by Dr Keshav Baliram Hedgewar on the auspicious occasion of *Vijayadashami* in the year 1925 at Nagpur. Dr Hedgewar, a born patriot and a freedom fighter, was a medical doctor but dedicated himself to the service of the nation. He was disgruntled on seeing the disorganised state of the Hindu society. With an intention to organise and restructure the Hindus, he founded the RSS.

[2] Founded in 1915, the Akhil Bharatiya Hindu Mahasabha was formed to protect the rights of the Hindu community in British India. One of the party's early leaders was the prominent nationalist and educationalist Pandit Madan Mohan Malaviya, who had also been a president of the Indian National Congress and worked closely with Gandhi. In the late 1920s, the Mahasabha came under the leadership of leaders, such as Balakrishna Shivram Moonje and Vinayak Damodar Savarkar—also known as Veer Savarkar. Savarkar disagreed with the ideologies of the Congress, and under him, the Mahasabha became a principal opposition to the Congress.

THE MEETING OF INTENTION

In 1944, while Gandhi was staying at Panchgani, in Maharashtra, a group of around 25 young men staged a protest against his policies. Another protest was organised against Gandhi while he stayed in the sweepers' colony in Delhi. Both the protests were carried out by the same men under the leadership of Narayan Dattatraya Apte.

A Brahmin from Pune, Narayan Apte was the son of Dattatreya Apte, a respected scholar and historian. Narayan earned his Bachelor of Science degree from Bombay University in 1932. After three years of unemployment, he was taken in as a tutor in Mission High School in Ahmednagar. He aspired to become a master in the field of education. He started a shooting club in Ahmednagar that gained a lot of publicity, after which he accepted a teaching job at Ahmednagar. It was during this time when he married Champa, the daughter of an influential family from Pune. He too wanted to contribute to setting India free from the British. In 1939, Narayan Apte joined the Hindu Mahasabha, where he met his ally Nathuram Godse.

Savarkar's *The Indian War of Independence* made its way to many revolutionary youths and eventually to Godse too. The book, which describes the 1857 revolt as a unified and national uprising of India as a nation against British authority, was seen at the time as highly inflammatory, and the Marathi edition was banned in British India even before its publication. Although this book was banned by the British administration, it was available for those who wanted it.

Godse and Apte found themselves gradually shifting from Gandhi's principles to the revolutionary ideas of Savarkar. They were deeply influenced by his principles, both wanting the Hindus to become a rigidly closed religious group. They gradually came to believe that Mahatma Gandhi supported the Muslim minority at the cost of the Hindus. Sarvarkar was arrested in 1910 for his connections with the revolutionary group India House. Following a failed attempt to escape while being transported from Marseilles, Savarkar was sentenced to two life terms—imprisonment totalling fifty years—and was moved to the Cellular Jail in the Andaman and Nicobar Islands, but was released in 1921 after several mercy petitions to the Britishers. In Ratnagiri jail, Savarkar wrote *Hindutva: Who is a Hindu?* Godse and Apte were radicalised by Savarkar's ideas and felt that Gandhi's way of working was anti-national. The two men were friends for six years and then became business partners. On 28 March 1944, they jointly started the publication of a Marathi daily for the Hindu Mahasabha, *Agrani,* in Pune, which was later renamed as *Hindu Rashtra.* Godse was the editor and Apte the manager.

THE CONSPIRACY

By early 1947, the Indian subcontinent stood on the verge of independence. People could feel that freedom would be granted by the imperial powers finally; it was just a matter of time now. However, a dark shadow was hovering over the nation. The idea of two nations—a separate nation for Muslims—was spreading like wildfire. A massive communal problem was emerging, and the partition of the subcontinent into two nation states seemed to be the only solution. Extremists among both Hindu and Muslim communities had developed a mutual distrust and hatred for each other. Several regions of the country saw a breakdown of law and order, resulting in riots. Although initially, the Congress opposed the proposal for the division of the country, consistent reports of riots and skirmishes among the two religious groups forced them to reconsider the idea. Muhammad Ali Jinnah, once a prominent member of the Congress and now the leader of the Muslim League, stood stubborn on his demand for a separate nation for Muslims. Congress members, failing to find an alternate solution, increased pressure on Lord Mountbatten, the last Viceroy of India.

Mahatma Gandhi stood firmly against the partition of the country, initiating another fast unto death. However, he was forced to discontinue it fearing that it may demoralise the nation. Nathuram learnt that Mahatma Gandhi had started a fast unto death to stop the Partition, but this did not change his attitude towards him. He detested Gandhi's belief in the oneness of God and the equality of all religions. Godse and his ilk considered these ideas to be at variance with their own Hindu beliefs. Various social reform programmes conducted by Gandhi, such as inter-caste marriages, highly distressed Godse who believed that Gandhi's actions always evinced a bias for minority groups.

After spending around 200 years in India[3], the British officially departed India on 15 August 1947. As the last act of imperial ruling, the subcontinent was divided into two independent nation states—India and Pakistan—initiating a transfer of population and property in both religious groups. The Partition brought havoc, tears and death. It triggered riots, mass casualties and a colossal wave of migration. Millions of people moved to what they hoped would be a safer territory, with Muslims heading towards Pakistan, and Hindus and Sikhs in the direction of India. Millions of people were eventually displaced—travelling on foot, in bullock carts and by train.

Estimates of the death toll post-Partition range from 200,000 to two million. Many were killed by members of other communities and sometimes their own families, as well as by the contagious diseases which swept through refugee camps. Women were often targeted as symbols of community honour, with up to 100,000 raped or abducted. Godse and Apte watched the Partition and the horrors that ensued. They believed that Gandhi was responsible for it. Gradually, their hatred towards him started turning into an insidious conspiracy to assassinate him.

On 13 January, at the beginning of what would prove to be his last fast, the Mahatma said, 'Death for me would be a glorious deliverance rather than that I should be a helpless witness of the destruction of India, Hinduism,

[3] Saurabh Chandra. 2015. 'The myth of 200 years of British rule in India', *Indian National Interest*, 14 November. Available at: https://nationalinterest.in/the-myth-of-200-years-of-british-rule-in-india-db74e183f5fb.

Sikhism and Islam', and explained that his dream was for the Hindus, Sikhs, Parsis, Christians and Muslims of entire India to live together in amity. At about five o'clock in the afternoon, the next day, the seventy-eight-year-old Gandhi, frail from fasting, was being helped across the gardens of Birla House. A huge crowd would gather to attend these meetings. On 30 January 1948, at the time of his evening prayer, a similar crowd waited for Gandhi. Unknown to all, would-be assailants Godse and Apte were a part of this crowd. He was running a few minutes late for the meeting but when he emerged—supported by Abha and Manu, his constant companions—he looked fragile. While Gandhi climbed the steps of the raised lawn where he conducted his prayer meetings, Godse stepped out of the crowd to block Gandhi's path, confronting him face to face. He bowed and pretended to touch his feet. Manuben objected to this. Godse quickly raised himself, took out a pistol in full view of the crowd and aimed it at Gandhi. The distance between the two men was minimal. Godse did not falter in his mission as he pulled the trigger and shot Gandhi squarely in the chest three times. Gandhi collapsed and fell on Abhaben's lap, murmuring, 'Hey Ram.'

Godse's radicalised mind had lost all rationality and was consumed with hatred for a man he had respected during his childhood.

THE END OF THE STORY

Nathuram Godse and Narayan Apte were arrested along with six others involved in the assassination of Gandhi. During the trials, the perpetrators showed no remorse, claiming their actions were committed for the sake of the nation. Godse's reasons for assassinating Gandhi included Gandhi's alleged attempt to sacrifice Hindu interests to appease minority groups and ultimately ended up blaming him for the Partition, which he believed could have been avoided. He recorded his reasoning in a 150-point statement, which he presented to the jury. Godse was kept in Ambala Jail and his trial lasted for over a year. He was sentenced to death on 8 November 1949 along with his co-conspirator Narayan Apte.

15 November 1949

Nathuram Godse emerged from his cell along with his companion Apte. As they were taken to the scaffold, Godse, in a hesitant voice, called out, '*Akhand Bharat*'. Apte completed his slogan by saying, '*Amar rahe*'. Those were the last words the men uttered. They were quiet after that till they were hanged.

Thus, the curtain fell on the first instance of capital punishment in independent India.

2

The Kairon Assassination

On the fateful day of 6 February 1965, Chief Minister of Punjab, Partap Singh Kairon, was killed in an attack. Along with the CM, three other people[1], who were travelling with him in his car, also lost their lives. The investigations led to the prosecution of three people—Sucha Singh, Baldev Singh and Nahar Singh. They were charged under Sections 120-B, 302, 302/34 of the IPC. The trial court found the accused guilty of the murder and sentenced them to death.[2]

BRITISH INDIA

Nihal Singh Kairon was a social reformer and a pioneer who was the first person in the province of Punjab to raise awareness for the education of women. He set up a girls' school in Patti and encouraged parents to send their daughters to school. He was a well-known and highly respected man in Amritsar.

On 1 October 1901, the Dhillon family was blessed with the birth of a beautiful and healthy baby boy. They named him Partap Singh. His father, Nihal Singh, laid

1 https://indiankanoon.org/doc/634895/.
2 https://indiankanoon.org/doc/634895/.

great emphasis on education and Partap was brought up on the same principles. After successfully completing his schooling in Amritsar, he went to Khalsa College in the city to pursue graduation. Nihal Singh was proud of his son and wanted him to achieve new heights and gain an education which could not be provided in British India. He thus decided to send him to the United States for higher studies.

Partap Singh took admission at the University of Michigan. Survival as a student in the US was difficult without adequate money, and the young man had to work hard to supplement his stipend. He started working in farms and factories while continuing with his postgraduate studies. Soon he passed out from the University of Michigan with a master's degree in political science. However, on completion of his degree, he did not immediately go back to India. He was impressed with the farming techniques the Americans deployed and was keen to learn it all, hoping to replicate those back home. He ended up spending ten more years studying farming methods, working on farms for 12 to 14 hours a day. When he was convinced that he had finally learnt it all, he decided to return to India.

It was 1929. Partap Singh had been deeply influenced by the American way of life. He envisioned a fruit-laden Punjab when he saw miles after miles of oranges, grapes and peaches in California. He believed that affluence on farms would be within the reach of Punjabi villagers only if they could have an independent government. He developed a pragmatic, determined approach to political, economic and social issues. When Partap

Singh reached his country, he was dismayed to find that nothing substantial had changed in all those years. The country was still under the grip of the British Empire; however, the foundation of the empire had slowly started weakening due to the number of protests seeking the end of the rule. His countrymen were now aware of an imperial power ruling them and their exploitation. Partap Singh wanted to do something to contribute to the revolutionary movement. He started an English daily in Amritsar on 13 April 1932 and named it *The New Era*. The newspaper became quite popular but as he soon entered active politics and could not give time to the newspaper, the publication was shut down. He initially joined the Shiromani Akali Dal (SAD), a party of Sikh activists. He was also a member of the Indian National Congress, the all-India party associated with the independence movement. As a Congress worker, he was jailed in 1932 for five years for participating in the Civil Disobedience Movement. He completed his jail term peacefully and returned to politics. His political career gradually evolved from 1941 to 1946, along with the freedom struggle in India.

On 8 August 1942, in the midst of the Second World War, Mahatma Gandhi launched the Quit India Movement at the Bombay session of the All India Congress Committee (AICC), demanding an end to British rule in India. The AICC launched a mass protest demanding what Gandhi called 'an orderly British withdrawal'[3] from India. Partap Singh, being an active

[3] https://www.mapsofindia.com/on-this-day/8th-august-1942-mahatma-gandhi-launches-the-quit-india-movement-in-mumbai.

member of the campaign, was again jailed in 1942 for his participation. The Quit India Movement was also quickly contained by the British; key leaders were arrested overnight without any trial. They were jailed for the remaining years of the war and thus had very little contact with the masses during this time. Sporadic, small-scale violence took place across the country, and the British arrested tens of thousands of leaders. In terms of immediate objectives, the Quit India Movement failed because of heavy-handed suppression, weak coordination among leaders and the lack of a precise plan of action. Although jail was not a new thing for Partap Singh, he was getting restless and was eager to secure his release. Finally, in 1945, when the war came to an end, he walked out free. One year after that, in 1946, he was elected to the Constituent Assembly of India.

POST INDEPENDENCE

At the time of independence, Partap Singh Kairon held offices in various state governments. He played different constructive roles over the years. Initially, he was elected as the rehabilitation minister and development minister between 1947 and 1949. The Partition had displaced over 14 million people along religious lines, creating a situation of overwhelming refugee crisis; there were large-scale violence, migration and chaos, with estimates of loss of life, accompanying or preceding the Partition, varying between several hundred thousand and two million. This was an extremely challenging situation and as the rehabilitation minister, he had to settle millions of refugees who had migrated from West Punjab amidst tremendous confusion. Kairon is credited with re-establishing millions in East Punjab not only with new homes but also with job opportunities. In a very short period of time, he provided stability for them in new professions to support themselves and their families.

In 1952, Kairon was at the peak of his political career, with being the rehabilitation minister and development minister between 1947 and 1949, and the chief minister of Punjab from 21 January 1956 to 23 June 1964. Even after seeing success and achieving political power, he never forgot his roots.

Kairon brought in prosperity for Punjab by preparing the ground for the Green Revolution and the growth of industries. He invited industrialists, such as the Oswals and the Jaijees, to invest in the state. Like his father Nihal Singh, Kairon firmly believed in the importance of education. He made primary- and middle-school education compulsory and free. He boosted higher education with the setting up of Punjab Agricultural University, Kurukshetra University and Postgraduate Institute of Medical Education and Research. He consolidated landholdings in undivided Punjab by pooling fragments of land into economically viable chunks—the only Indian state to do so—thus preparing farms for mechanisation.[4] The law that was passed for this helped farmers in not only improving their produce but also bringing them relief from confrontations with each other. A villager by conviction and an American by

[4] https://www.hindustantimes.com/punjab/builder-of-punjab-the-lost-legacy-of-sardar-partap-singh-kairon/story-LgBkUb0ttLrpMYISj2o9zH.html.

education, Kairon was always looking for opportunities to help the farmers of his state.

Partap Singh Kairon was considered one of the most progressive chief minister of the state. According to M Rajiv Lochan, Panjab University, Chandigarh, Partap Singh succeeded in restoring communal harmony, opposing both the Punjabi Suba Movement and the language movement.[5] With the introduction of innovation, Punjab was placed on the industrial map of India. Further, The Partition had also cost the state its original capital—Lahore. It now needed a new capital. Renowned American planner and architect Albert Mayer was tasked to design a new city called Chandigarh in 1949. Kairon, during the years of his chief ministership, helped in the creation of Chandigarh, which was completed in 1960. He also helped in establishing the industrial township of Faridabad, now the largest city in the state of Haryana and a major industrial hub.

Punjab became the first state in India to have electricity in all its villages. The state's basic requirement of infrastructure in terms of irrigation, electrification and roads were fulfilled. Everything was going well until a disaster struck.

THE REIGN ENDS

The first blow was dealt in 1964, during his second term as the chief minister. Corruption charges were levelled

---

[5] https://www.hindustantimes.com/punjab/builder-of-punjab-the-lost-legacy-of-sardar-partap-singh-kairon/story-LgBkUb0ttLrpMYISj2o9zH.html.

against him. There were three probes, however, he was absolved of all three. A month after Prime Minister Jawaharlal Nehru's death in May 1964, Kairon resigned after being charge sheeted by the Das Commission. It's a measure of the high standards in public life those days that one of the charges Kairon, a severe diabetic, faced was of taking along a government doctor while travelling.[6] Kairon was a man of vision, a man of strong likes and dislikes and the allegations were a serious blow to him; he thus resigned from his position as the chief minister of Punjab.[7] Nobody knew at that time that he was not only resigning from his post but also from his life.

At the same time that a conspiracy was being hatched by three assassins with Sucha Singh as their ring leader. Their target was Partap Singh Kairon. Sucha Singh was convinced that Kairon had played a crucial role in the conviction of two culprits in a murder case, Ajit Singh and his father Bir Singh. They were in custody and under trial. When they were convicted Sucha Singh, probably closely connected to the convicts, believed that Kairon had taken a personal interest in securing the conviction of both the criminals.[8]

On 6 February 1965, while on his way from Delhi to Chandigarh, he was waylaid near Rasoi village, Rohtak district. Sucha Singh and his friends Baldev Singh and Nahar Singh had been following them and

---

6 Ibid.

7 https://www.hindustantimes.com/punjab/builder-of-punjab-the-lost-legacy-of-sardar-partap-singh-kairon/story-LgBkUb0ttLrpMYISj2o9zH.html.

8 http://www.sikhiwiki.org/index.php/Pratap_Singh_Kairon.

seized the opportunity when it was presented to them. They took out their guns and started shooting at the car. Their target had been travelling with his personal assistant, an IAS officer and his driver. Partap Singh Kairon was assassinated on the spot along with his co-passengers.

Sucha Singh, Baldev Singh and Nahar Singh were hanged to death in 1969.

The Kairon family still flourishes in Punjab politics and is one of Punjab's promnent political families. Kairon's grandson Adesh Partap Singh Kairon, who is married to the daughter of Parkash Singh Badal has been twice a minister under the chief ministership of his father-in-law Parkash Singh Badal, and his son Surinder Singh Kairon was a member of the Indian Parliament. His younger son Gurinder Singh Kairon has also been actively taking part in politics as a member of the Congress. While his third child, his only daughter, Sarbrinder Kairon has actively supported her nephew and brothers in all of their political endeavors. Partap Singh Kairon placed Punjab on the industrial map of the country. He was behind the creation of the city of Chandigarh and the industrial township of Faridabad.

3

Ranga and Billa

THE DAY BEFORE THE HANGING

30 January 1982
Tihar Jail, New Delhi
Five journalists stepped into the dreaded Tihar, one of the largest prison complexes in South Asia. Amongst them, was renowned journalist Prabha Dutt who had recently petitioned the Supreme Court of India to be allowed to interview death row convicts. Dutt, the chief reporter of the *Hindustan Times,* had initially requested the jail authorities for permission to interview them but her request was rejected. She decided to challenge this decision at the highest court in the land. In a landmark judgement for *Prabha Dutt vs Union of India,* 1982, the apex court directed the superintendent of Tihar Jail to allow representatives of a few newspapers to interview two death sentence convicts, Ranga and Billa.[1]

Ranga and Billa, sentenced to death for the kidnapping and gruesome murders of two children, had shaken the nation and led to a massive furore. Even

[1] Peu Ghosh, *Indian Government and Politics* (New Delhi: PHI Learning, 2017).

the then prime minister, Morarji Desai, had taken a keen interest in the case. When Dutt and the other reporters from *The Times of India, India Today,* Press Trust of India and United News of India walked in, they were taken towards the far end of the jail where the convict was being held, close to the gallows. There they saw him, behind the iron grills, watched over by a sentry. The gallows, close to his cell were awaiting him, where he was about to be taken the next morning.

It was Billa.

Ranga had refused to be interviewed.

THE CRIME THAT SHOOK THE NATION

26 August 1978

16-year-old Geeta Chopra was a second-year student in Jesus and Mary College, New Delhi. Her brother, Sanjay, 14 years old, was in the 10th grade, studying in Delhi's renowned Modern School. Their father, Madan Mohan Chopra, was a captain in the Indian Navy, and the family lived in the Officer's Enclave in Dhaula Kuan.

On that fateful day, Geeta and Sanjay were supposed to participate in a radio programme called the Yuva Vani on All India Radio (AIR). The programme was supposed to air at eight in the evening and the siblings were to reach the AIR office on Sansad Marg by 7 PM.[2] It was decided that their father would pick them up outside the office at 9 PM. Geeta was to compere the programme while Sanjay would be a participant. An

[2] http://womenjust.weebly.com/blog/1978-geeta-chopra-rape-and-murder-or-ranga-billa-case

intelligent young girl, Geeta was fond of sports, dance and Western music. Sanjay, on the other hand, enjoyed music and dreamt of joining the navy like his father. The family on this Saturday evening were thrilled as they would hear their children on the radio. The children bade their farewells around 6:15 PM; their mother wished them luck and cautioned them to be safe.

Geeta and Sanjay were on their way to the AIR office when they saw a mustard coloured Fiat car coming towards them. The car stopped next to them and they could see that there were two men inside. They offered the siblings a lift and as it was drizzling, Geeta and Sanjay agreed. As luck would have it, the men were no ordinary people. They were Kuljeet Singh, aka Ranga, and Jasbir Singh, aka Billa—hardened criminals who were, as police investigation would reveal later, wanted by the Bombay Police and had fled to Delhi.[3] When they saw the children, they thought they belonged to a rich family and kidnapped them hoping for ransom.

When they were inside the car, the two men locked the vehicle. On realising that they were trapped, Geeta and Sanjay raised an alarm. Billa threatened them with a small kirpan. Sanjay tried to snatch the kirpan but was injured in the attempt.

Gole Market Intersection
6:30 PM

Bhagwan Dass, the owner of an electrical goods store, was riding towards North Avenue on his scooter. When he reached the Gole Market intersection a car drove past him

[3] Now Mumbai

dangerously. It was a mustard coloured Fiat bearing the registration number HRK 8930. As the car passed him, he heard some noises coming from inside. A girl was crying for help. He sensed that something was not right. Someone was in danger. While trying to catch up with the car, he saw two teenagers sitting in the back seat of the car. One of them was a girl who was pulling the hair of the driver while the other was a boy shouting angrily at the person in the passenger seat. However, before he could get any closer the car sped away towards Willingdon Hospital.[4] Dass knew something terribly awful was happening and immediately telephoned the police control room in North Delhi. He gave them the car's licence plate number, but it was wrongly noted by the operator as MRK 8930. Dass also reported that the girl was shouting for help. His report was recorded at 6:44 PM.

Near Willingdon Hospital

Inderjeet Singh Noata, a junior engineer at the Delhi Development Authority (DDA), was going home on his scooter. When he was just about to reach Willingdon Hospital, a car suddenly overtook him. The driver seemed to be in a tearing hurry and this made Noata suspicious. He decided to follow the car and sped behind it. He could see a boy in the back seat with his face pressed against the window. The boy was waving his hands, crying for help and his T-shirt seemed to be stained with blood. Noata also saw a young girl, next to the boy, pulling the driver's hair. Having seen enough to know that this meant trouble, he decided to chase

[4] Now Dr Ram Manohar Lohia Hospital.

the car further. However, the car accelerated when it reached the crossing of Mandir Marg and Park Street,[5] jumped the red light and vanished. Noata had noted the car registration number and immediately called Rajinder Nagar Police Station. The car number was recorded correctly this time. Police officials recorded his statement around 6:45 PM.

Police Control Room, North Delhi
7:05 PM

Following up on the complaint by Bhagwan Dass, Sub-Inspector Om Parkash left for Gole Dak Khana on his motorcycle along with a constable at 7:05 PM. He reached the spot as reported by Bhagwan Dass. But by the time he reached, no one was present to tell him what had happened. After making enquiries with a few passers-by, he returned to the police station.

Rajinder Nagar Police Station
7:40 PM

The station house officer (SHO), Ganga Swarup, noted down the report by Inderjeet Singh Noata. They initially dismissed the case, stating that the incident took place in the jurisdiction of the Mandir Marg police station, and the case had to be handled by them. The officers relayed Noata's report to the police control room as well as the Mandir Marg Police Station.

---

[5] Now Sheikh Mujibur Rahman Road.

Meanwhile…
Ranga, who had seen Dass chasing them, was spooked and suggested dropping the kids off and fleeing. Billa, however, refused. They parked their car near Buddha Jayanti Park and changed the car's license plate. The new number was DHI 280.[6] They asked the siblings whether they wanted something to eat or drink. Sanjay asked for water and was offered a cola. He refused it initially. He was then offered an ice cream, which he accepted on his sister's suggestion. When Ranga and Billa asked the children about their parents, they discovered that their father was a naval officer. They panicked after learning this. First, it meant that their father wouldn't be able to pay a huge ransom. Second, Ranga was afraid that the father might want to take them on. Ranga again suggested that the kids should be let off but Billa refused.

Billa managed to trick the children into staying in the car, saying that they would let them go and drove the car on. After some time, they stopped the car and took Sanjay about 100 yards away from the vehicle. Billa forced Ranga to attack the boy with a longer kirpan which was later retrieved from their belongings. After one blow, Ranga couldn't continue, and Billa snatched the kirpan and repeatedly struck Sanjay. Sanjay died on the spot.

Billa and Ranga then took turns to rape Geeta. In a last effort to save herself, Geeta injured Billa on the head with the kirpan, but she was killed too. The duo

[6] Investigation later revealed that the duo had several spare car number plates.

abandoned the bodies of the children in the nearby bushes and fled the scene.

Officer's Enclave
8:00 PM
Madan Mohan Chopra and his wife tuned in to AIR to listen to the voices of their children. When the programme started, they heard an unfamiliar voice. It was a girl's voice, but it definitely wasn't their daughter. Thinking they might have tuned into the wrong channel, Mr Chopra adjusted the radio to make sure he had tuned in to the right one. His wife wondered whether the programme had been shifted to some other time slot or another day. Mr Chopra realised that he would not get the answers by sitting at home. He got up to visit the AIR office.

AIR Office
Sansad Marg
9:00 PM
At the AIR Office, Chopra found out that his children were not there. He was extremely worried now. When he checked with the officials, he was told that they never arrived. As Geeta and Sanjay were unavailable, the AIR had to find replacements for the show. Mr Chopra rang up his wife to inquire whether the children had reached home. Mrs Chopra said that they had not. Mr Chopra could feel the ground beneath his feet shaking. He decided to go back home on his scooter. On the way, he kept a keen eye on the street for his kids.

Officers Enclave
Past 9:30 PM

Captain Chopra reached home and together with his wife started enquiring about his children in the neighbourhood, hoping that they might be with their friends and relatives. With each call, their hearts sank. Everybody said that Geeta and Sanjay hadn't visited them. When they ran out of options, they decided to go to the police. Captain Chopra, around 10 PM, rang the police central control room and informed them that his children were missing. Minutes later, a police patrol car arrived at the Chopra residence. The worried father climbed in and a search of hospitals, homes of friends, restaurants and the more deserted parts of the city was conducted.

Willingdon Hospital
10:15 PM

As Billa had suffered an injury to his head, both of them visited Willingdon Hospital. When the doctor asked for patient details, they used false names and cooked up a story to justify the injury. They said they were attacked and robbed near Kali Mandir in Baba Kharak Sing Marg. They claimed Billa's head injury resulted from being hit with an iron rod. The constable on duty at the hospital took their statement and forwarded the report to Mandir Marg Police Station. They left the hospital at 11:10 PM on the doctor's advice, accompanied by two policemen. The police asked Billa and Ranga to take them to the location where they were supposedly robbed. When they reached the alleged spot, the two policemen failed to find any evidence of the robbery or any signs of any struggle.

Mandir Marg Police Station
01:45 AM

Billa and Ranga were about to leave the station after giving all the details to the officials when they were asked to report to the station in the following morning. They agreed to the officer's demand and left the station.

28 August 1978
Midnight

Head Constable Rohtas Singh was conducting his daily night patrol around the Delhi Ridge. His job was to prevent crime and illegal activities occurring under the blanket of darkness. The head constable was unaware that it was going to be a long night. As he was crossing the ridge, a cowherd informed him that he had seen two dead bodies at the Ridge while grazing his cattle in the evening. The constable immediately rushed to the ridge to verify this and found the bodies of a girl and a boy. He quickly informed his seniors. Based on the reports received at the Central Control Room from Rohtas Singh, the officials at Rajinder Nagar Police Station were soon informed of the incident. The sub-inspector of Rajinder Nagar Police Station, Hari Chand,[7] along with other police officers, visited the location where the bodies were found. In order to determine whether this was connected to the

[7] https://en.wikipedia.org/wiki/Geeta_and_Sanjay_Chopra_kidnapping_case#cite_note-GHOSH2012-12

kidnapping case reported two days ago, Hari Chand asked his officials to request Captain Chopra to report to the location of the bodies.

Captain Chopra and his wife reached the location as per the police instruction, terrified of what they might find. Hari Chand was waiting for them, he informed the couple that the police had discovered the bodies of a young girl and boy and asked them to identify whether the bodies were in fact of their children. Mrs Chopra broke down on hearing this—it seemed as if their worst fears might come true. For the last couple of days, their lives had been a dark scary tunnel, waiting for a ray of light and now suddenly everything seemed to be coming to an end. Gathering whatever courage was left in them, they saw the bodies.

They were Geeta and Sanjay indeed. The Chopras were stunned, forced to face the terrible truth—their two precious children were dead.

The sub-inspector's suspicions were correct. There were 25 stab wounds on Sanjay's body, most of them on his right arm. Sanjay was a boxer and had obviously fought bravely to the bitter end. Geeta's body carried six stab wounds, mostly on her chest, head, her left palm and a gaping slash across the neck.

4:30 AM

Sub-Inspector Hari Chand sent his report to Rajinder Nagar Police Station. A case was registered under Section 302 of the IPC. After the crime team had inspected and photographed the crime scene, Hari Chand held an inquest on the dead bodies of Geeta and Sanjay and sent them for a post-mortem examination. The post-mortem report established the time of death between 7 PM and midnight of 26 August.

THE CAPTURE

8 September 1978
Kalka Mail Train

As the Kalka Mail slowed down on the Yamuna Bridge before entering Agra, two men barged into a compartment. Unfortunately, for Ranga and Billa, the compartment was reserved for military personnel. Lance Naiks Gurtej Singh and AV Shetty stopped them and asked what they were doing there. One of them lied that they were also from the army. When they were asked to show their identity cards, Ranga and Billa started acting strangely. The military men suspected that the two might be robbers or thieves and decided to hold on to them. This resulted in a scuffle between them and the army personnel apprehended the two, tying them with ropes. The army men still did not know the real identity of the intruders until Lance Naik turned the pages of the Hindi newspaper *Nav Yug* that he was carrying. He came across a photograph of a man whose face resembled one of the intruders he had just captured. They now knew that this was much more than what they had expected. Lance Naiks proceeded to question the duo. The intruders admitted that they were in fact, Billa and Ranga. Singh and Shetty realised that they had captured two of the most wanted criminals in the country.

9 September 1978
Delhi Main Station, 3:30 AM
The military personnel handed over the suspects and their handbags to Inspector VP Gupta, SHO, Delhi Railway Main. They were produced before DIG Shri Mander within a few hours and ultimately brought to New Kotwali for interrogation.

THE AFTERMATH

When the two heavily manacled criminals were eventually escorted to New Kotwali, a huge crowd had gathered to catch a glimpse of them. The intention of the enraged crowd was clear. They wanted to lay their hands on both the killers. If a massive police force had not been present, Ranga and Billa would have been killed by the angry mob. The enraged citizens demanded that the culprits be hanged publicly, but the law had to be followed.

After a few hours of police interrogation, both culprits confessed that they had committed the murder of the Chopra children. They later retracted their confessions during the trial giving rise to speculations that the confession might have been coerced. Ranga and Billa had already stated that murdering the children was never their plan. They only stabbed the children because of the unexpected resistance they put up. After killing them both, they dumped their dead bodies on the ridge. Later, they went to a hospital to get Billa's scalp wound, which he had received during the scuffle with Geeta in the car, treated.

The appellants were charge-sheeted for various offences. The trial judge charged the appellants under IPC Sections 365/34, 364/34 and 366/34. Each one of them was individually charged under IPC Section 376. Two charges—under IPC Sections 302/34—were also framed against them for committing the murder of Sanjay and Geeta respectively.[8]

4 YEARS LATER

31 January 1982
Kuljeet Singh (alias Ranga Kush) and Jasbir Singh (alias Billa) were hanged to death in Tihar Jail on 31 January 1982. According to reports, Billa was quiet but Ranga had resisted the gallows. Their bodies were not claimed by their relatives.

LEGACY

In 1978, the Indian Council for Child Welfare instituted two bravery awards for children under the age of 16, the Sanjay Chopra Award and the Geeta Chopra Award, given each year along with the National Bravery Award. The Kirti Chakra was awarded by the Government of India to both Geeta Chopra and Sanjay Chopra on 5 April 1981.

[8] For the complete report see, https://indiankanoon.org/doc/1359524/.

4

Maqbool Bhat

THE KIDNAPPING OF A DIPLOMAT

3 February 1984

Birmingham, England

Indian diplomat Ravindra Hareshwar Mhatre was the second-ranking official in India's consular office in Birmingham. Today was a special occasion—it was his daughter Asha's birthday. As he stepped out of a bus, carrying a birthday cake for Asha, suddenly, out of the blue, a dark shroud obstructed his vision and before he could even figure it out, he was kidnapped. The kidnappers sent out a message that they wanted only one thing from the Government of India—the release of a man who was imprionsed in Tihar Jail, a man who was very important for them, their former leader Maqbool Bhat.

KASHMIR: THE UNREST AND THE BIRTH OF A MILITANT

1938–46: Years before the Kidnapping

In the village of Trehgam, Handwara tehsil, Kupwara district, Jammu and Kashmir, there lived a peasant family.

Ghulam Qadar Bhat and his wife were poor and used to struggle to meet ends. On 18 February 1938, they had a son and named him Maqbool Bhat. The harsh living conditions in Kashmir, the unforgiving climate and the diminishing crop yield, affected Maqbool's family, as it did the rest. Kashmir was under the feudal rule of the Dogra family. The king would allocate portions of his land to those loyal to him and who would help him in suppressing his subjects. The loyal supporters, known as *jagirdars,* were made owners of large landholdings or *jagirs*. The *jagirdars* would not work directly on the land. It used to be the task of the peasants, who would plough the land, sow the seeds and harvest the crops. Suppressive and feudalistic, during harvest time, the *jagirdars* would appropriate a majority of the produce, leaving the bare minimum for the peasants. This was the harsh reality of the peasants.

One season, due to particularly poor weather, there was in widespread crop failure. The peasants could not give the crop share and consequently, the *kardars,* who were agents of the *jagirdars,* harassed the peasants, beat them and raided their homes and grain stores. The peasants pleaded before a *jagirdar* when he arrived at the village, explaining the reasons for the low production levels. However, the *jagirdar* did not relent and asked them to stay hungry and arrange for his share of grains. As he went back and sat in his car after delivering the order, hundreds of peasant children prostrated themselves in front of the vehicle. The peasants pleaded with him to either stop the further collection of grains or to crush these children while he left. The car could not move an inch. Hearing the cry of the hungry and naked children lying in front of him, he agreed to their terms. Maqbool was among these children, and the cries and pleas he heard that day was something he would never forget. The Dogra rule not only shaped his political awakening but also led him to pursue a path rife with danger and uncertainty—a path of political activism and struggle for Kashmir's independence from the dominions of India and Pakistan.

When Maqbool was in a primary school in his village, during award ceremonies, parents of the affluent children and that of poor children were seated separately. One year, when Maqbool was also one of the awardees (passed matriculate in 1945), he refused to receive the award until that 'class segregation' was not scrapped. The tradition was thence changed. He, along with many other youngsters, protested for the school to be raised to the secondary level and even helped in building it after the order was released.

Despite significant struggles, Maqbool was keen to pursue his education. After completing his schooling in Trehgam, he took admission in St Joseph's College, a private missionary college in Baramula, where he earned a bachelor's degree in history and political science. An articulate man, Maqbool was a frequent speaker during his college days. His fiery campus speeches about the Plebiscite Front led to his college principal stating, 'If he manages to pass through the hardships, this young man will become a great man.'[1] The principal's words were

---

1 https://freepresskashmir.com/2018/02/12/chapter-two-what-fuelled-kashmirs-maqbool-butt.

almost prophetic. Maqbool also continued his reading on religion, a practice he had been following since childhood. He would gather people from his village in his room or near a spring close to his home and teach them about Kashmir, his audience would mostly comprise his acquaintances, students and those who were not well read. Abdul Ahmed Shah, a local from Trehgam, said, 'Maqbool used to make them all sit in a line there. He had a small blackboard on which he used to draw Kashmir and explain how we were all slaves.'

In 1957, Maqbool gave his graduation exams at an examination centre in Srinagar. Sheikh Abdullah had been released from jail around the same time (December 1957), which had led to a chain of massive protests against the government. Student activists were arrested, after Sheikh was rearrested on 27 April 1958. Maqbool was an obvious target because he was heading the student activists of Plebiscite Front during those days. He went underground for three months, requesting his father to bring the temporary certificate when his results were announced. Maqbool stayed out of the public eye until the results were declared and then left for Pakistan with his uncle, Aziz Bhat.

Maqbool, Aziz and a few more men left on foot towards Pakistan through Teetwal but were arrested after their crossover and sent to a police station in Muzaffarabad. When asked why he had crossed over, he said that it was impossible for him to stay in a slave-nation, so he had no other choice. His uncle explained the situation of Kashmiris on the other side of the border. A few friends of his uncle, Ghulam Nabi

Zargar and Ghulam Nabi Mir, who had crossed over to Pakistan-administered-Kashmir during the Partition somehow heard about them and secured their release. In 1958, Maqbool and his family decided to leave India and settled in Peshawar, where they met Sohbat Khan, an old friend of Aziz Bhat. Sohbat Khan worked at Peshawar University and helped Maqbool in getting admission there for Urdu Literature. Maqbool soon joined a local newspaper, *Anjaam*, to earn a living and express his thoughts. His uncle soon left for India-administered-Kashmir to get his wife. His relatives requested him to also bring Aziz's sister, Raja Begum, along with him. Aziz returned with both of them and stayed at his master's house for a few days. During that time, Maqbool expressed his desire to marry Raja Begum and Aziz agreed. They got married in 1961 and had two sons—Javed Maqbool and Showkat Maqbool. Javed Maqbool was born in 1962. In the same year, Kashmir Independence Committee (KIC) merged with into the Jammu Kashmir Mahaz-Rayee-Shumari—Plebiscite Front in Azad Kashmir—which was a crusade for complete independence of Kashmir from India. Showkat Maqbool was born in 1964. But Raja Begum fell severely ill and was unable to move around. Fearing what would happen to his children, Maqbool married again in 1966 to a school teacher Zakira Begum, and had a daughter Lubna Maqbool from her.

Maqbool Bhat was a Kashmiri freedom fighter and co-founder of the Jammu Kashmir Liberation Front. He was a leading voice of the struggle for freedom among the Kashmiris. His politics came into conflict with the state machinery of the India-administered-Kashmir. It was at this time when he led several agitations for the political rights of the people of Kashmir.

Maqbool Bhat formed Jammu Kashmir National Liberation Front (JKNLF) along with Amanullah Khan on 13 August 1965. Maqbool Bhat, Amanullah Khan, Aurangzeb and Kala Khan crossed the division line to India-administered-Kashmir in June 1966. The purpose was to explore the feelings of Kashmiris there with the possibilities of forming cells there. It appeared that during the three-month tour of JKNLF guerrillas in different towns and cities, they managed to convince some people that an armed struggle for national liberation was the only way to liberate Kashmir.

Most of the Kashmiri record on the history of JKNLF and Maqbool Bhat shows that on their way back, they were intercepted by Indian intelligence agencies. In a clash with one of the security teams, Aurangzeb died. Maqbool Bhat and Kala Khan were arrested on 14 September 1966.

30 January 1971

On 30 January 1971, at 1:05 PM, an Indian F27 friendship aircraft named Ganga, flying from Srinagar to Jammu, landed at Lahore airport under the control of two hijackers, Hashim Qureshi and his cousin Ashraf Qureshi, who were apparently armed with a hand grenade and a pistol. It was discovered that they were armed with toy weapons which were anything but lethal (the hand grenade was made of wood and the Pistol was just a toy). The aircraft carrier, apart from the crew (four in all, including the Captain), had 26 passengers. The two hijackers demanded the release 36 political prisoners, said to be members of the JKNLF, from the Government of India. They also demanded that the families of the two hijackers in Kashmir would in no way be harmed.

On 2 February 1971, at about 7:00 PM, Khurshid, who was the personal secretary to Mohammad Ali Jinnah from June 1944 until Jinnah's death in 1948, was told that the situation was tense and that Pakistan International Airlines (PIA) had stopped its daily supply of food to the hijackers. Maqbool Bhat arrived in Lahore from Peshawar. The hijackers Hashim and Ashraf had demanded Bhat to meet them. Sardar Abdul Vakil Khan, the then superintendent of police (SP) in Lahore, took Khurshid and Maqbool to a room where Hashim sat with some other officials. He told Bhat that the hijackers were demanding that he set fire to the plane. As Khurshid and Maqbool were being escorted out, the SP said, '*Khuda ke liye hamari jaan chhorh do, jahaz ko urha do*'.

The 'hijackers' were lauded as heroes of the freedom struggle of Jammu and Kashmir in Lahore. All the passengers were released and were allowed to go back to India, and subsequently, Ganga was set on fire by the hijackers on upon the advice of SP Sardar Wakil.

A few weeks later, when India reacted by banning the passage of Pakistani aircrafts over India, the same heroes were then seen as villains. Authorities in Pakistan had arrested the hijackers and 150 other activists of JKNLF. Six among them were tried in a special court of Pakistan under charges of collaborating with the Indian intelligence services. They were Maqbool Bhat, GM Lone, Mir Abdul Qayyum, Mir Abdul Manan, and the two hijackers, Hashim Qureshi and Ashraf Qureshi. Maqbool Bhat was released in 1974. Hashim Qureshi was sentenced to fourteen years in prison. However, he was released in 1980 after he won his appeal in the Supreme Court of Pakistan.

ENTRY INTO INDIA AND ARREST

In May 1976, Maqbool Bhat once again crossed over to India, even though he was advised against it. On 7 June 1976, Indian forces spotted and arrested him in Langate, a tehsil in Kupwara district of Jammu and Kashmir, India. His first operation, a bank robbery in Langate, intended to raise funds, went badly wrong. A bank manager was killed and Bhat was arrested. He was held in New Delhi's Tihar Jail. Outside, supporters of Bhat had already hatched a plan.

Mohammed Aslam Mirza and other members of the JKLF kidnapped Ravindra Mhatre, a 48-year-old diplomat at the Indian High Commission in Birmingham. He was bundled into a car and taken to a makeshift 'prison' at a house in nearby Alum Rock. There, he was held against his will for two days until the late afternoon of 5 February. He was driven to a really remote spot in Leicestershire (51.5 kilometres away) and, in that isolated spot, he was shot three times. Mhatre was murdered after letters were sent to news agencies demanding a ransom of a million pound and the release of Maqbool Bhat from Tihar Jail in India.

Prime Minister Indira Gandhi responded by promptly executing Bhat. Two of the JKNLF kidnappers were found guilty by a British court for having carried out Mhatre's execution, and received life sentences in February 1985. The third kidnapper, Mohammad Aslam, succeeded in evading the authorities until July 2003, after which he was detained in the United States.

Two First Information Reports (FIRs) were registered against Maqbool Bhat. The first one was lodged at Sopore Police Station, Kashmir (FIR 84/66) charged Maqbool Bhat for crossing the ceasefire line without a valid legal permit and with an illegal purpose of overthrowing the lawfully established government of Jammu and Kashmir. The second FIR filed at Panzala Police Station, Kashmir (FIR 38/66) charged Maqbool Bhat with the murder of Amar Chand. It alleged that Bhat and his accomplices took cash, ornaments and other documents from CID (Crime Investigation Department) Inspector Amar Chand's house, and then abducted and killed Amar.

Maqbool Bhat, in his defence, denied all charges against him, except for crossing the ceasefire line in June 1966 without a valid legal permit. According to his account, it was not necessary to carry a permit for moving around in his own country. At the end of the cross-questioning, the Supreme Court found him guilty and delivered a death sentence. Maqbool Bhat, however, had petitioned the president of India for clemency on the grounds of an unfair trial. The judgment, delivered on 6 August 1982, observed that in view of the mercy petition pending before the president, Bhat could not be classified as one 'under sentence of death'. Therefore, he could not be in confinement. The court held that his transfer to the death cell on 27 April 1981 was 'arbitrary and illegal'.

But after the abduction and murder of Ravindra Mhatre, the Indian Government was in no mood to spare Maqbool Bhat. The president of India, Giyani Zail Singh, rejected Bhat's mercy petition.

Maqbool Bhat was hanged on 11 February 1984 in Tihar Jail in New Delhi.

5

Satwant Singh and Kehar Singh

On 6 January 1989, Satwant Singh and Kehar Singh, convicted for the assassination of Prime Minister Indira Gandhi, were hanged in Delhi's Tihar Central Jail. It was the culmination of the most sensational murder case ever in India, which had been wending its way through various courts over four years. Quite in contrast to the trial of Nathuram Godse and Narayan Apte, who were hanged within 22 months of killing Mahatma Gandhi, the verdict was slow in coming.

Kehar Singh was convicted of conspiring with Beant Singh who, along with Satwant Singh, had shot Indira Gandhi dead on 31 October 1984. Once their deaths was confirmed, their bodies were cremated on a platform built in the jail premises, specifically for this purpose. All the arrangements had been made for a swift execution and cremation.

TRACING BACK: BEANT SINGH

Beant Singh was born to Sucha Singh and Kartar Kaur on 8 May 1950 in Maloya, a village near Chandigarh,

Punjab. After completing his primary education at the local village school, he studied for a short time at Hameerpura and finished his schooling from Khalsa School. He then joined Panjab University, Chandigarh, and earned a Bachelor of Arts degree in 1970. He also completed his diploma in Russian from the same university. After completing his education, he moved to Delhi in 1972 to look for employment. It was in Delhi, where he trained and became a part of the Delhi Police. He became a sub-inspector in the Delhi Police and worked in the security branch of the Central District and North Delhi areas.

During his service in the Delhi Police, Beant Singh stayed in Vishnu Garden, a Sikh-dominated locality, in West Delhi. His uncle Kehar Singh too lived in Delhi and worked as an assistant in the Directorate General of Supply and Disposal. He had a good relationship with his uncle and used to visit him often. On 23 January 1976, he married Bimal Kaur. They lived a happy married life and the couple had three children—Amrit Kaur, Sarbjeet Singh and Jaswinder Singh. With his nephew now a family man, the two families—Beant Singh's and Kehar Singh's—became closer with frequent visits to each other's house.

TRACING BACK: SATWANT SINGH

Satwant Singh was born on 23 January 1976 to Tarlok Singh and Piar Kaur in the village of Agwan Kurd in Gurdaspur district, which is only three kilometres away from the India–Pakistan border. Satwant Singh had two elder brothers, Gurnam Singh and Waryam Singh, a younger brother, Swaran Singh, and a younger sister, Ranjit Kaur. Satwant Singh went to a higher secondary school called Dera Baba Nanak School.

In 1981, Satwant Singh moved from Burail Jail in Uttar Pradesh to a new posting with the Delhi Armed Police. He was an excellent sharpshooter. As a result, he was later posted to the personal protection force of the prime minister. From the period of 1981 to 1984, he was the personal bodyguard of Indira Gandhi. It was during this time that he became acquainted with Beant Singh. In 1983, Sarabjit Kaur, the wife of his elder brother Waryam Singh, asked her *masi* (maternal aunt) for her daughter's hand for marriage to Satwant Singh. Soon both of them were engaged. Both families had scheduled the wedding in 1984, but due to the fact that Satwant Singh could not get holidays, it was delayed.

OPERATION BLUE STAR

Indira Gandhi, daughter of the country's first prime minister, Jawaharlal Nehru, was a formidable politician and is the only woman prime minister of India so far. Born in 1917 to the famous Nehru family, she served as the prime minister from 1966 to 1977 and from 1980 until her assassination in 1984. While her stints were marked with numerous landmark achievements and progressive decisions, she was also accused of centralisation of power and political ruthlessness. She declared a state of emergency in India from 1975 to 1977.

THE KHALISTAN MOVEMENT

It is the religious–political movement within Sikh groups for the creation of a separate state of Khalistan. From the late 1970s, it assumed a militant demeanour. The Akali Dal indirectly supported the movement and created a charter of demands. Though the resolution did not explicitly call for a separate country, it envisioned transfer of territory to Punjab, as well as a considerable devolution of power from the Centre to the state of Punjab. But it was one Jagjit Singh Chauhan who first supported the idea of an independent Sikh country. Chauhan was said to be in constant touch with Bhindranwale, and the former held some radical ideas of a separate Sikh state. Bhindranwale was a leader of the Damdami Taksal—a Sikh religious authority and a political revolutionary in the early to mid-1980s.

Bhindranwale pioneered the demand for the independent Sikh nation of Khalistan. Bhindranwale was initially supported by the Congress during the late 1970s. The Congress backed Bhindranwale to weaken the Akali Dal in Punjab and split the Sikh vote. The Congress supported the candidates backed by Bhindranwale in the 1978 SGPC (Shiromani Gurdwara Parbandhak Committee) elections. The Congress leader, and ex-President of India, Giani Zail Singh allegedly financed the initial meetings of the separatist organisation, Dal Khalsa. The association of Bhindranwale with the Congress increased his influence and stature in politics. Bhindranwale and his supporters increasingly came to be associated with acts of violence. In the early 1980s, there were a series of murders in

Punjab. In 1981, a journalist and Congressman named Lala Jagat Narayan was found murdered, allegedly at the behest of Bhindranwale's men. Narayan had been advocating against the use of Punjabi in Hindi schools in Punjab and the acceptance of Hindi instead of Punjabi by Hindus living in Punjab. Bhindranwale had earlier been a suspect in the murder of the Nirankari leader Gurbachan Singh, who had been killed on 24 April 1980.

The Punjab government arrested Bhindranwale but later released him for the lack of evidence. By this time, the Akali Dal, which had been considering Bhindranwale as a Congress agent, began to make a common cause with him. This might have irrevocably changed Bhindranwale's equation with the Congress and Indira Gandhi.

The Akali Dal and Bhindranwale launched the Dharam Yudh Morcha in August 1982. It called for the implementation of the Anandpur Sahib Resolution[1]. Prime Minister Indira Gandhi, however, viewed the document as a secessionist one and took an aggressive stand. Agitations of the Morcha were violently suppressed by the police. Over 30,000 Sikhs were arrested. The supporters of Bhindranwale continued with violent acts of murders and bombings in Punjab. Bhindranwale's influence made it difficult to even arrest those people.

In June 1984, Bhindranwale and his armed supporters took refuge inside the Amritsar Harmandir Sahib Complex, which housed the Golden Temple. Negotiators failed to convince Bhindranwale to abandon the hideout.

---

1 The Anandpur Sahib Resolution was a statement with a list of demands made by Punjab political party, the Shiromani Akali Dal, in 1973.

Despite the presence of civilians in the temple complex, Indira Gandhi ordered the Indian army to enter into the holy shrine to carry out Operation Blue Star.[2] From 1 to 6 June 1984, Indian army troops systematically attacked the militants hiding in the Akal Takht with tanks, artillery, helicopters, armoured vehicles and tear gas—all mobilised to remove Jarnail Singh Bhindranwale and his armed followers. The heavy and focused attack was successful; Bhindranwale's was one of the 42 bodies found inside the temple premises. The Indian army had suffered 331 casualties. Bhindranwale was dead but this came at the cost of the lives of innocent civilians who were trapped in the temple crossfire. Indira Gandhi's orders and the military action, especially the demolition of Akal Takht, was conceived as sacrilegious and sparked a huge uproar amongst the Sikh community not only in India but worldwide. The assassination of Indira Gandhi, in turn, led to an anti-Sikh pogrom, where around 3000 Sikhs were killed. The act was viewed as an unparalleled tragedy in Indian political history. Sikh sensibilities were also offended at the alleged entry of army personnel with boots into the temple complex and the alleged destruction of Sikh scriptures and manuscripts in the temple library that caught fire due to explosives used during the operation. Such claims and other rumours led to an atmosphere of mistrust towards the government. Many Sikhs resigned from the armed and civil administrative offices and several people returned awards and honours they had received from the Indian government. According

---

[2] For more details about Operation Blue Star and the Khalistan Movement, see https://www.thequint.com/explainers/khalistan-golden-temple-operation-bluestar-anniversary

to government figures, 493 militants and civilians were killed in the operation. Indira Gandhi's political image was tarnished heavily and she was severely criticised for the operation that eventually led to her death.

THE AFTERMATH

In ten years of service to the prime minister, Beant Singh had earned a reputation for being a dutiful bodyguard. But the sheer loss of lives and the assault to the Sikh faith that happened because of Operation Blue Star severely distressed him. The violence and devastation distressed him immensely and he held his boss, Prime Minister Indira Gandhi, entirely responsible. Days after the operation had been carried out, he visited Sri Darbar Sahib. The effects of the massacre had scarred the temple complex; he could feel the pain and hear the cries of innocents killed there, an agony that was unbearable. This experience made him much more devoted to his religion. Gradually, a fervour took over. His wife often noticed how his voice trembled during the time of *ardaas*.

During that difficult time, his uncle Kehar Singh attempted to counsel him, teaching him about Sukha Singh and Mehtab Singh. Kehar told Beant how these two legendary figures took *amrit*[3] from Sahib Sri Guru Gobind Singh and then went on to take the head of the military commander Massa Rangar to stop the desecration of Sri

---

[3] *Amrit Sanchar* (also called *Khande di Pahul*) is the Sikh ceremony of initiation or baptism. The *Amrit Sanchar* is the initiation rite introduced by Guru Gobind Singh when he founded the Khalsa in 1699. A Sikh who has been initiated into the Khalsa is titled 'Amritdhari' or 'Khalsa' after Singh (man) or Kaur (woman).

Darbar Sahib. The story had a tremendous impact on him and sowed the seeds of revenge.

THE ASSASSINATION

Beant Singh was looking for a partner in crime, who would sacrifice all just like those legendary men who avenged the action on Sri Darbar Sahib. Eventually, Beant Singh's eye fell on Satwant Singh, who was in Indira Gandhi's protection force with him. When he carefully approached Satwant Singh, the young Singh responded by saying, 'Elder brother, for this sacred task, not only this life but even if I have to sacrifice several lives, I would kill a brutal murderer like Indira Gandhi!' Once the plan to eliminate the prime minister was made, Beant Singh and Satwant Singh wanted to see with their own eyes what havoc did Indira Gandhi wrecked in the temple of Amritsar. The scene at Sri Akal Takht Sahib, shocked and pained them and convinced them of the righteousness of their decision. So they went to Sri Darbar Sahib and did *Ardas*—'Oh Akaal Purkh, give us strength!'

The group returned to Delhi the following day, three days before Diwali. It was a day on which Indira Gandhi used to distribute gifts and sweets to her staff and security personnel. Beant Singh and Satwant Singh, however, refused the gifts from her. This was their way, perhaps, of distancing themselves emotionally from the person they had hitherto been loyal to.

31 October 1984

In order to execute their plan, Beant Singh and Satwant Singh had to be together on duty while guarding Indira

Gandhi. Satwant Singh was assigned a late shift while Beant Singh worked the early shift. They had to devise a way so that they were both on duty at the same time.

On the morning of 31 October 1984, Satwant Singh, as usual, was assigned as the security personnel at Gate No. 4 at the Akbar Road House. He had been issued a SAF Carbine (Sten-gun) along with 5 magazines and 100 live rounds of 9 mm ammunition. Claiming that he was suffering from indigestion, he managed to get someone to take his place and got himself posted at the TMC Gate which was nearer to the restroom.

The prime minister, on that fateful day, had an engagement with Peter Ustinov—an acclaimed actor and writer. He wanted to interview her for an Irish documentary that he was working on and his crew was ready with the equipment. They were waiting at the home office of the prime minister at Akbar Road. The official residence of the prime minister, which was on Safdarjung Road, was connected to her home office by a narrow cemented pathway.

At about 9:10 AM, Indira Gandhi emerged from her house with Head Constable Narayan Singh just behind her holding an umbrella to protect her against the sun. Her personal security officer Rameshwar Dayal, her personal attendant Nathu Ram and Special Assistant RK Dhawan were closely following her as she was on her way to meet Ustinov.

When Gandhi, at the head of the entourage on the cemented pathway, approached the TMC Gate both Beant Singh and Satwant Singh were waiting for her. Beant Singh was armed with his service revolver while

Satwant Singh held his SAF carbine. The moment Gandhi reached the TMC Gate, Beant Singh fired five rounds at her. When she collapsed on the ground, Satwant Singh proceeded to fire 25 more rounds. As the prime minister fell on the ground, the duo dropped their respective weapons and shouted in unison, 'We have done what we needed to, now you can do what you have to.'

The Indo-Tibetan Border Police commandoes, who were guarding the premises, immediately apprehended the two and waited for their senior officers to arrive and interrogate them. As they were waiting, there was an altercation between the commandos and the assassins. Satwant Singh grabbed a handgun from one of the other bodyguards and, in response, the other commandos opened fire at the two of them. Beant Singh was shot dead and died on the spot while Satwant Singh was seriously injured.

When the senior officers arrived, Satwant Singh was taken to Dr Ram Manohar Lohia Hospital, about five kilometres away. Doctors operated on him, removing two bullets from his abdomen. Beant Singh, on the other hand, was declared dead by the doctors. Indira Gandhi, meanwhile, had been taken to All India Institute of Medical Sciences (AIIMS) in a white ambassador accompanied by her daughter-in-law Sonia Gandhi. Head Constable Narain Singh filed an FIR at the Tughlaq Road Police Station at 11:25 AM. The doctors at AIIMS did their best to revive Indira Gandhi, using 40 bottles of blood as her liver, lungs and kidneys were bleeding profusely. Nevertheless, around 1:00 PM the prime minister of India was declared dead.

The news of Indira Gandhi's demise was announced in the evening on Doordarshan and her elder son, Rajiv Gandhi, was sworn in as the sixth prime minister of India. This news resulted in violent retaliation and mob uprising against the Sikh community all over the country. Thousands of Sikhs lost their lives, and the national capital witnessed the worst of the killings and destruction which lasted for about four days.

ARRESTS AND TRIALS

Kehar Singh was a religious fanatic. He had an intense hate against Prime Minister Indira Gandhi for causing damage to the Akal Takhat in Golden Temple. He was in a position to influence Beant Singh, being the uncle of Beant Singh's wife. He converted Beant Singh, and through him Satwant Singh, to religious bigotry. He also took Beant Singh to Golden Temple in Amritsar on 20 October 1984. It is alleged that Balbir Singh, an accused conspirator, had expressed his resentment openly, holding Indira Gandhi responsible for 'Operation Blue Star'. He was planning to commit her murder and had discussed his plans with Beant Singh, who had similar plans to commit the murder. He also shared his intention and prompted Satwant Singh to commit the murder of Prime Minister Indira Gandhi and finally discussed the matter with him on 30 October 1984. In the first week of September 1984, when a falcon happened to sit on a tree near the reception area of the prime minister's residence at about 1:30 PM, Balbir Singh spotted the falcon, called Beant Singh there and pointed out the falcon to him. Both of them agreed that it had brought a message of the Tenth Guru of the Sikhs and that they should do something to revenge Operation Blue Star. Therefore, both of them performed *Ardas* then and there. Balbir Singh was posted on duty at the Prime Minister's residence. On 31 October 1984, his duty was to commence in the evening. When reported for duty in the usual course, he was asked to go to security lines. At about 3:00 AM on 1 November 1984, his house was searched and a book on Bhindranwale was recovered. At about 4:00 AM, he was taken to Yamuna Velodrome and kept there till late evening. Thereafter, on December 1984, he was said to have been arrested at Najafgarh Bus Stand where he was searched and certain articles were recovered from his possessions that included a piece of paper containing certain entries described as 'memorandum events'. It was allegedly written by him. After the investigation, a charge sheet was filed against appellants Satwant Singh, Balbir Singh and Kehar Singh.

They were subjected to interrogations and trials.[4] Kehar Singh and Balbir Singh were charged for being the conspirators of the assassination. The Supreme Court held that the case against Balbir Singh was false. During their interrogation, Satwant Singh consistently denied any conspiracy behind the assassination and asserted that he and Beant Singh had acted alone. The

---

[4] For a detailed report of the trials see, https://indiankanoon.org/doc/667073/.

case went to trial like any other case under the Indian legal system.

Additional Sessions Judge Mahesh Chandra tried their case and found the three of them guilty of all the charges that were made against them and sentenced them all to death. Satwant Singh was given additional sentences as well. They appealed to the High Court of New Delhi, but the High Court confirmed the verdicts and sentences passed by the trial court.

When the case went to the Supreme Court, the sentences of Satwant Singh and Kehar Singh were sentenced to death once again. Balbir Singh, on the other hand, was acquitted of all the charges in August 1988. While Balbir Singh walked a free man out of the apex court, the other two convicts filed a mercy petition, their last resort. Their mercy petition was rejected by President R Venkatraman.

Before the sentence could be carried out, a controversy arose. Satwant Singh, his legs paralysed with a bullet in his spine, had been held under guard in the Ram Manohar Lohia hospital while recuperating from multiple gunshot wounds received during a struggle with other security guards following the killing. The question was whether an injured person could be hanged. Satwant Singh underwent an operation and the bullet was successfully extracted from his body. Once it was ensured that there was no health hazard to Satwant Singh, both men started to count their days.

There was no sleep for a restless Satwant Singh the night before his hanging. He finally dozed off for about an hour around 4:00 AM.[5] According to jail wardens, his condition worsened in the morning but he was still hoping that a stay order would come until the very end.

THE FINAL DAY

The morning of 6 January 1989 was cold and wintry. The families were not even allowed to come near the jail premises that morning. Satwant's family had stayed quietly in their rooms adjacent to the historic Sisganj Gurdwara in Old Delhi. But Kehar's stepson Rajinder Singh, who had tirelessly worked for his father's defence for the past four years, was there with his mother, Jasbir Kaur, and five brothers. Around 7:30 AM, both men were finally taken to the gallows. They stood silent and mute at the sight of the gallows, watching the hangmen examine the knots, which would soon be tightened around their necks. The family started wailing and shouted out—'*Jo bole so nihal, sat sri akal*'. Rajinder shouted slogans like—'Shahid Kehar Singh *amar rahe*'. His distraught aunt quickly clamped her hand over his mouth as he started to shout 'Rajiv Gandhi *murdabad*'. The family's main concern was getting Kehar's body and they petitioned to the Supreme Court. The next day, Chief Justice RS Pathak and Justice MN Venkatachalliah sat at the former's residence to hear it. G Ramaswamy,

---

[5] https://www.indiatoday.in/magazine/indiascope/story/19890131-indira-gandhi-assassination-trial-satwant-singh-and-kehar-singh-hanged-815690-1989-01-31.

representing the State, said that the ashes had already been collected by the jail staff that morning.

The judges then ordered that Satwant's father Tarlok Singh and Rajinder along with one of his brothers be taken along when the ashes were taken for immersion.

Both Satwant Singh and Kehar Singh were declared martyrs by the Shiromani Gurdwara Parbandhak Committee (SGPC) and the Unified Akali Dal.

6

Harjinder Singh and Sukhdev Singh

Operation Blue Star in the summer of 1984 and the anti-Sikh riots that followed Prime Minister Indira Gandhi's assassination on 31 October 1984 left a trail of blood and violence. Indiscriminate violence against the Sikh community in Delhi, and in others parts of the country, in the first week of November 1984 led to a loss of hundreds of innocent lives. Independent sources estimate the number of deaths at about 8,000–17,000 while government estimates project that about 2,800 Sikhs were killed in Delhi itself. This mob uprising was led by prominent politicians affiliated to the ruling party which further led to deep distrust and resentment of the Sikhs against the government. The Khalistan movement—a Sikh separatist movement calling for the creation of Khalistan which was to serve as a homeland for Sikhs[1]—which had started in the 1970s and grew in momentum in 1980s, amassed many Sikh supporters in the aftermath of the aforementioned events. Among

---

[1] For more details on the Khalistan movement and Operation Blue Star, see https://www.thequint.com/explainers/khalistan-golden-temple-operation-bluestar-anniversary

them were Harjinder Singh 'Jinda' and Sukhdev Singh 'Sukha', two men who devoted themselves to the movement and were behind one of the biggest bank robberies that India had ever witnessed. But it was their involvement in three high-profile killings that sent them to the gallows.

THE TURNING POINT

Gadli, Amritsar
Punjab

Gulzar Singh and Gurnam Kaur were blessed with their fourth child on 4 April 1962. They named the newborn Harjinder Singh. Jinda had two elder brothers, Nirbhail Singh and Bhupinder Singh, and one sister, Balvinder Kaur. The family were Gursikhs and hardworking farmers. Harjinder completed his school education in Gadli district. Later, he joined Khalsa College in Amritsar, where he pursued his graduation. When Operation Blue Star happened in 1984, Harjinder was in the second year of college. Under the orders of Prime Minister Indira Gandhi, the Indian army entered the premises of the Golden Temple, Amritsar, with tanks, artillery, helicopters, armoured vehicles and tear gas in order to remove militant religious leader Jarnail Singh Bhindranwale and his followers from the Harmandir Sahib Complex. The destruction of Akal Takht and the killing of innocent civilians trapped in the temple complex led to a huge uproar in the Sikh community in India and worldwide. This event radically changed Harjinder who decided to avenge the death of the innocent people. He decided to dedicate his life to the cause of the Khalistan movement.

Chak N: 11 Ganganagar
Rajasthan

Sukhdev Singh was born to Mengha Singh and Surjeet Kaur on 14 August 1962. He completed his early education in Manakpur, a village in Patiala, Punjab, along with the daily study of the Gurbani. He dedicated himself to the understanding of the power of wisdom and the conscious mind. After completing his schooling, he joined Gyan Jyoti College, where he earned his graduation degree and further enrolled for post-graduation. Operation Blue Star had an immense impact on Sukhdev as well. Like the other members of his community, he was hurt and enraged. He too discontinued his education and left home on a mission to avenge the deaths of his people.

FATEFUL ENCOUNTER

Harjinder was visiting his maternal grandparents, who lived in Chak, when he met Sukhdev Singh. The men became good friends as they shared their stories and experiences. Both of them had found someone who shared their ideals and goals. They vowed to avenge the death of their Sikh brothers and sisters killed in Operation Blue Star.

Since the preparations for the operation had taken place in Delhi, they decided to make the capital the hub of their activities. Soon both men became subjects of suspicion. Their photographs were broadcast on television. Despite this, the duo managed to escape the police a number of times. Harjinder Singh was arrested in Gujarat but he managed to hoodwink the police and escape while he was being taken to court. With each daring escape, they were resolved to plan bigger.

THE ASSASSINATIONS AND HEIST

1985

New Delhi

Soon, a chain of assassinations shook the pillars of the Indian government. The targets were identified with the help of a booklet titled *Who Are the Guilty?*, published by two organisations: People Union's for Civil Liberties (PUCL) and People's Union for Democratic Rights (PUDR). The list included 227 people who led the mob killings of the Sikhs. Congress MP Lalit Maken's name was third on the list. Maken was allegedly involved in the burning down of a gurdwara and spreading panic.

On 31 July 1985, Lalit Maken was moving towards his car parked across the road from his house in Kirti Nagar, New Delhi. His wife Geetanjali and a visitor, Balkishan, were standing at the gate of their house. Maken was about to unlock his car when he was shot at by three gunmen—Harjinder and Sukhdev Singh, along with another accomplice, Ranjit Singh—from a distance. Maken's wife started screaming as her husband fell. The three of them continued firing. Maken's attempt to take cover in his house failed and the bullets found their mark. Maken died on the spot and the three assailants escaped on their scooters. Geetanjali and Balkishan were caught in the firing too and did not survive.

A month later, on 5 September 1985, Congress leader Arjan Dass, also held responsible by the assassins for his role in the anti-Sikh riots, was murdered. Harjinder and Sukhdev managed to evade arrests for some time. However, Interpol arrested their accomplice and co-conspirator Ranjit Singh, who had fled to the US, in New Jersey on 14 May 1987.

1986

Pune, Maharashtra

General Arun Vaidya was the Chief of the Indian Army during Operation Blue Star in 1984. One of India's most decorated officers, he retired on 31 January 1986, after completing over 30 years of service. As the principal organiser of the operation, he was well aware of being a high-profile target for assassins but never regretted his participation. Stating in an interview earlier he had mentioned: 'I do not see any difference in taking up arms against a foreign enemy or an enemy from within. One who takes up arms against his own brother-citizens, against his own Constitution and legally constituted government is enemy enough, deserving the most ruthless punishment.[2] After retirement Vaidya settled in Pune.

On 10 August 1986, around 11:45 AM, Vaidya and his wife were driving home from a market on Rajendrasinhji Marg after a shopping trip. Harjinder

---

[2] https://www.indiatoday.in/magazine/cover-story/story/19860831-former-army-chief-general-a.s.-vaidya-assassinated-by-sikh-militants-in-pune-801208-1986-08-31

Singh and Sukhdev Singh were closely following the couple on their scooters. They pulled up next to Vaidya's car and fired at the car. Police investigations revealed later that four reportedly clean-shaven men pulled up alongside the car on motorcycles, with the lead assassin firing three shots at Vaidya through the window on the driver's side. The first two bullets penetrated his brain and killed him instantly. His car steered towards a cyclist named Digamber Gaikwad, and the cycle was crushed, though the cyclist escaped unharmed, the general's car stopping in front of a compound wall. A third bullet struck Vaidya on the shoulder, with another striking his wife Bhanumati in the neck. His bodyguard, who was also in the car, was wounded by four bullets in his back and thighs. The bleeding general was carried to the Command Hospital in a passing green matador van, and was declared brought dead.

Harjinder and Sukhdev Singh had crossed out another name from their hit list.

After assassinating Vaidya, Sukhdev Singh returned to Pune once again to gather the weapons that his co-conspirators had left behind. On 17 September 1986, he was riding his motorcycle on the roads of Pune when he collided with a truck. The accident not only injured him but led to his arrest. During the interrogation, Sukhdev named Ranjit Singh as the third accomplice in the assassination of Lalit Maken. Within the haunting silence and darkness in jail, he hoped that his friend Harjinder would continue their mission.

Sukhdev's confession brought Ranjit Singh under the police scanner but he had, by then, fled to the US. He was later arrested by the Interpol, in New Jersey, on 14 May 1987. On receiving the news, the Indian government began the proceedings to extradite Ranjit to India.

1987

Ludhiana, Punjab

Harjinder Singh and his co-conspirator General Labh Singh of the Khalistan Commando Force had planned something big as the next move. On 13 February 1987, disguising themselves in police uniforms, they headed to the Miller Gunj branch of the Punjab National Bank in Ludhiana with a group of Sikh militants. The plan was to rob the bank and use it to fund the Khalistan movement. They cleverly managed to cross a police check post and reached their planned destination.

It was a regular working day for the employees at the bank. Suddenly, 12 to 15 Sikh men marched into the bank, dressed as policemen, and armed with guns and rifles. Without inflicting any injuries, they conducted a clean robbery, looting a whopping sum of Rs 5.70 crore. This operation stands as one of the biggest bank robberies that India has ever witnessed.

ARRESTS AND TRIALS

A year after the bank robbery, Harjinder Singh made the mistake of coming to Delhi. This time around the police were prepared for him. They confronted a weapon-less Harjinder and during the brief encounter, he was shot in the leg. He was finally arrested near Gurdwara Majnu Ka Tila in March 1987.

Meanwhile, in New Jersey, a federal magistrate approved the extradition of Ranjit Singh on 6 February 1988. However, his return to India was delayed for another two years and he was finally extradited to Delhi in February 2000. He was held in Yerwada Central Jail, Pune. He was awarded life imprisonment in 2009, but the sentence was commuted by the then chief minister of Delhi, Shiela Dikshit, after Lalit Maken's daughter, Avantika Maken, gave her consent. Ranjit Singh walked out of jail as a free man on 7 July 2009.[3]

Harjinder and Sukhdev Singh were found guilty of the assassination of General Vaidya, Lalit Maken and Arjun Dass. A designated court within the premises of the Yerwada Central Jail conducted the case. They were acquitted on charges under Terrorist and Disruptive Activities (Prevention) (TADA) Act but were convicted under charges of the Indian Penal Code. During their court trial, despite admitting to the killing, they pleaded not guilty. They were given death sentences on 21 October 1989.

Harjinder and Sukhdev Singh refused to appeal their convictions. They declared that no petition should be filed on their behalf. Despite their wishes, Senior Counsel HS Phulka filed a mercy petition just a day before their hanging. The cabinet held an emergency meeting asking for the mercy petition to be rejected, and the President of India Shankar Dayal Sharma did so.

While imprisoned, Harjinder and Sukhdev wrote many letters documenting their feelings about their

---

[3] For more information see, https://scroll.in/article/766615/anti-sikh-riots-how-a-daughter-forgave-her-fathers-killer

days in jail.[4] They did not want to wear jail uniforms. Instead, they wanted to be hung wearing *kesri dastaars*, *cholas* and *kacherras*. Their letters suggest that they were impatiently waiting for their judgement day to arrive.

THE LAST DAY

9 October 1992

Yerwada Central Jail, Pune

On the day of their hanging, both Harjinder and Sukhdev woke up at 12:00 AM. After taking their baths, they went on to do their regular prayers before being led towards the gallows. On the way, they thanked the jail officials for keeping them for five long years. They shouted *jaikaras*[5] all the way. The two of them slowly climbed the gallows. There were four deputy police commissioners, 10 assistant police commissioners, 14 inspectors, 145 sub-inspectors and 1,275 officers assigned to prevent any sudden Sikh militant attack and ensure that the execution was carried out smoothly. With their respective nooses simultaneous They shouted *jaikaras* one final time before they breathed last at 4:00 AM.

---

[4] For the letters see, http://panthicdal.com/panjab-news/international-panthic-dal-urges-all-sikhs-to-remember-our-great-shaheed-singhs/

[5] *Jaikara* is a compound word, combining *jai* (meaning success or victory) and *kar* (meaning an action taken). Therefore, *Jaikara* is an act or utterance in a symbolic show of strength and achievement. Both these words are part of the Sikh terminology and have often been used in the Sikh religious literature, especially in the Guru Granth Sahib.

7

Auto Shankar

The 1980s were coming to an end.

Madras,[1] a bustling city on the coast of the Bay of Bengal in South India, was emerging as the second capital for movie business after Bombay. Kollywood, as the locals called their film industry, was flourishing. One of their own, Marudur Gopalan Ramachandran, popularly known as MGR, was at the pinnacle of power as the chief minister of the state. However, lurking under the glitz and the glamour of the city was a shadow of crime and terror—a serial killer who left many seaside villages in the grip of terror. In the end, all that was left was a man behind bars, desperately hoping that the president of India would accept his mercy petition.

THE RISE OF A CRIMINAL

In the early 1980s, Tamil cinema progressed into one of India's leading film industries. People were inspired, movie stars were venerated as gods and the youth wanted to be like the men they saw on the screen. Selling dreams and the aspiration of making it big has always been the craft of moviemaking. Amongst the millions

[1] Now Chennai.

who dreamt to make it to the silver screen was Gowri Shankar.

Born in 1955 at Kangeyanallur village in Vellore district, Shankar grew up as a movie buff. In 1974, like many others from the middle- and low-income groups of the time, he moved to Madras, the city of his dreams, to find a job. He settled in Periyar Nagar where he found work as a painter, but the money was not enough. Shankar was obsessed with movies and wanted a break in the industry, but when he failed to do so he started driving auto-rickshaws.[2] The money was decent and the job helped him learn his way around the city better.

Madras was still a growing city in those days quite small in comparison to what it is today. The bustling seaside suburb of Thiruvanmiyur was then, only a sleepy fishing hamlet. The entire coastline from Thiruvanmiyur to the ancient town of Mahabalipuram was a string of fishing villages with coconut and palm plantations in between. Well-constructed roads were practically non-existent, if not, mostly in a bad condition. Police patrol was minimal.[3]

Through the 1970s and early 1980s, Tamil Nadu had implemented and repealed prohibition twice. The state was a booming market for bootleggers. The coastal hamlets were the perfect location to brew *arrack* or country liquor. Palm trees gave a plentiful supply of toddy as well. It was an industry where one could make a quick buck if one didn't mind the risk. Small autos could navigate streets easily and could pass through almost the entire city unnoticed. It was the

---

[2] https://www.awaaznation.com/social-issues/auto-shankar/

[3] http://www.bodahub.com/auto-shankar-serial-killer/

perfect distribution mechanism. It was during this time Shankar got involved in bootlegging to earn some quick bucks. He started buying *arrack* for a small amount and selling it for a heftier sum in the city.

Shankar soon earned a reputation in the world of crime. After all, crime and its lure too can be magnetic and Shankar had gotten a taste of it. He formed a gang of his own to help consolidate his new business. Members of his gang included his younger brother 'Auto' Mohan, Jayavelu, Rajaraman, Ravi, Palani and Paramasivam. As his main associates, he had Eldin, his brother-in-law and Shivaji. His gang quickly rose to fame and was soon ruling the entire Thiruvanmiyur area. They made it the hub of their illegal activities, which included bootlegging and gradually delved into the flesh market. He trafficked poor women from the seaside hamlets and ran brothels in the slums of Periyar Nagar and at a lodge on L.B. Road. His autos were used as transport for both his businesses—trading illicit liquor and exploiting young women in the burgeoning flesh trade.

THE REIGN OF RED

In the year 1988, nine young girls were reported missing in Thiruvanmiyur. The police initially thought that the girls were sold into prostitution by their parents. But the parents kept denying the allegations and insisted on further investigations. After six months of relentless demands of the parents, the police began a serious and thorough investigation. The truth was something else. Shankar and his gang had abducted the girls for his prostitution racket.

Shankar was the leader of the gang which was thriving on *arrack* trading and ran brothels which were illegal and harmful to the society. He was responsible for spoiling the lives of many girls. He used to keep some of the girls for himself and had set up a separate residence to hold them. These girls were subjected to cruelty at the hands of Shankar who used to burn the young girls with cigarette butts. A girl named Sundari unable to bear the torture committed suicide by setting fire to herself. Lalitha, another girl forced to stay with Shankar, one day managed to escape with one of his confidantes, Sudalaimuthu who used to send women to the customers and collect the money received for Shankar. On learning this, a furious Shankar decided to make the couple pay the price for their betrayal. They were tracked down by his goons and brought before Shankar. Lalitha was clubbed to death and the gang buried Lalitha's body in a vacant plot in Periyar Nagar. Her remains were not discovered for the next 15 months. Her lover Sudalaimuthu had started a brothel business separately and reportedly used to take Shankar's customers to his brothel house and had thus incurred the wrath of Shankar. Sudalaimuthu was brought into Shankar's house to be killed. The body was burnt and the remains were thrown away in the sea. Likewise, it was alleged that Ravi, who was making enquiries about Sudalaimuthu was also murdered and his body was buried in a pit dug near his house.

Shankar's influence and audacity kept growing as did his victim count. During his reign of terror, a major political crisis gripped the state. Tamil Nadu suffered a major loss in the death of Chief Minister MGR in

December 1987. Following his death, the state faced an immense political vacuum. With law and order at stake, Governor's Rule was imposed between 1988 and 1989. Governor PC Alexander was put in charge of maintaining law and order. The governor directed Jaffer Ali, deputy inspector general of police of Chennai range, to form a new team of policemen. It included inspectors Thangamani and Ranganathan from Pallavaram circle, sub-inspectors, Subramanian and Sengeni, and constables, Rajan Babu, Natarajan, Devadas and Perumal with Aari, a constable from the neighbouring Tiruvannamalai district, who was very well known to Shankar.

Shankar's gang was growing and it naturally pulled him into gang wars. In one incident, the gang confronted three men name Mohan (not his younger brother), Sampath and Govindaraj from a rival gang, whom Shankar had accused of trying to snatch a woman of his from a lodge at L.B. Road. The confrontation escalated to a gruesome fight.

On 29 May 1988, Shankar's brother-in-law took Anita, a prostitute from Shankar's brothel to V.G.P. Golden Beach and told them that she should be returned at about 3 PM to the cashier. Mohan, Sampath and Govindaraj were drunk at this point of time when they saw Anita and caught hold of her. Anita panicked and cried for help. Eldin questioned them but they threatened him. At about 3:30 PM, Paramasivam arrived at Palani's house where Babu, Shankar and Shivaji were playing cards, to inform Shankar about the incident. He also told them that Eldin had been beaten up by three men from Mandhaveli and that they had misbehaved with Anita as well. All of them rushed to the 29th Cross Street brandishing Casuarina poles from the shed of the *arrack* shop of Mohan. Shivaji beat the auto driver in whose auto the three men were travelling. The driver, however, escaped with his auto. Thereupon, Shankar and his associates surrounded the three men and attacked them. Meanwhile, Shankar's driver was asked to go to Mandhaveli to find out whether the men they were beating up were from Mandhaveli. Shankar's assumption was right; they were from Mandhaveli. Shankar felt that the matter was starting to get out of hand and decided to remove the three injured persons to his house. They were taken in an auto to the Shankar's house. He also threatened the residents in the locality not to reveal this to the outsiders. The three injured men were held inside the storeroom and it was locked. At about 10 PM, Mohan opened the storeroom and found that two of them were already dead and one was groaning in pain. He was dragged from the storeroom and was strangled to death. They buried the bodies separately. Two of them in one place and the third one at another location.

A relative of the deceased Mohan went to Thiruvanmiyur Police Station on 31 May 1988 and orally reported about the missing men. The circle inspector, sent them away saying that the constable told him that no such incident has taken place. The witness went to Abiramapuram Police Station and gave the complaint. The sub-inspector registered a 'Man missing' case and took up the investigation. On 7 June 1988, 15 reports about the missing men had been reported to the DSP Parangimalai. As a result of the subsequent investigations, Babu was arrested. Shankar was arrested too but was later released on bail.

The police gradually shifted their focus from Shankar and the gang continued trying to expand their operations by kidnapping young girls. In one such attempt, in December 1988, a girl name Subalakshmi was passing through a wine shop. An auto-rickshaw slowly crossed her, and the driver tried to abduct her. She was almost pulled into the auto but managed to escape. Shankar had failed this time; the girl lodged a complaint with the police. As police officers studied her complaint, they started looking for the auto driver whom she had described. A team of police went undercover to the wine shop and managed to learn more about the dreaded auto driver, a man who, according to rumours burned his victims after killing them. The nickname Auto Shankar originated around this time.

IN PRISON AND A DARING ESCAPE

Babu, during the interrogation following his arrest, gave a confessional statement at Pallavaram police station. On the basis of this confession, the police started looking into Shankar again, which soon led to him being arrested a second time. This time around, he made a confessional statement. His house at Gandhi Road was searched for incriminating evidence. In fact, Babu and Shankar directed the police to the dead bodies.

The police recovered a total of five bodies from Periyar Nagar. Lalitha's remains were dug out during this time. This news spread like wildfire and caused a sensation among the residents. During the raid, they also seized his diary, which contained photographs of a number of policemen across ranks posing with him, revealing the power he wielded over the law enforcement. The government acted swiftly and the concerned policemen were suspended immediately.

As the case went to trial Babu turned approver and helped in convicting the culprits. On 31 May 1991, Shankar, Eldin and Shivaji were sentenced to death at Chengalpattu Sessions Court.[4] Five other accused in the case—Jayavelu, Rajaraman, Ravi, Palani and Paramasivam—were awarded life imprisonment. During the trial, Shankar initially stated that it was cinema that had turned him into a criminal. When the case went to the High Court of Madras, Palani and Paramasivam were acquitted of all the charges. The court confirmed the remaining charges on 17 July 1992.

Although Shankar had confessed to his crimes, he was not planning to stay in prison for long. On the night of 20 August 1992, Shankar and his gang members had a few visitors in their cell. Three jail officials entered their cell and did not lock the cell as they exited. It is unclear whether it was an act of negligence or by design. The next morning the cell was empty. Shankar and his friends had managed to escape from prison. After the incident, an embarrassed government suspended twelve junior-level officials and jail wardens. The jail management was forced to face the government and the media after the incident. The officials were determined now to save face

[4] For complete details of the trials see, https://indiankanoon.org/doc/1593993/

and tracked down Shankar in Rourkela, the steel city in Orissa[5] and he was brought back to prison once again. Following his capture, the jail wardens who helped him escape were sentenced to six months of imprisonment.

The gang was rounded up and tried for the murders of Lalitha, Sudalai, Sampath, Mohan, Govindaraj and Ravi committed in a span of two years. The victims were either burnt after being killed or were buried inside residential houses.

As the day of their execution came closer, the convicts appealed to the Supreme Court hoping for a lighter sentence. Justice KJ Reddy and GN Ray dismissed their appeal on 5 April 1994. Shankar's last option was the president of India. He filed a petition to President Shankar Dayal Sharma for clemency. This plea was rejected too.

On 31 May 1991, their fates were sealed by the Supreme Court. Shankar was hanged to death in Salem Prison at 05:14 AM on 27 April at the age of 41.

Auto Shankar and his associates were the last convicts to be hanged in Tamil Nadu.

[5] Now Odisha.

8

Dhananjoy Chatterjee

Sexual violence is a dastardly act. With increasing reports of sexual violence now streaming on our televisions and printed in the papers, as a society, we are now more aware of the deep malaise that runs through our society. A lot of these incidents stem from a lack of security, infrastructure and proper preventive systems. But what happens if the person who is supposed to protect you becomes a violator? Or the one who is there to guard you is the one who hurts you? When you think about it, it almost shakes the foundation of trust of every relationship human beings value. This trust was shaken and broken for an innocent girl on 5 March 1900 in Kolkata.

It was a usual day for 18-year-old girl Hetal Parekh. A student of the reputed Welland Gouldsmith School, Hetal returned to her home in Bhowanipore after giving an exam. It was afternoon and when she stepped into the apartment, she found that her parents were not at home. Though what happened next did not have a witness, the aftermath of those few hours not only devastated the Parekh family but left the city of Kolkata stunned. When Hetal's mother Yashmoti Parekh returned home from a visit to the temple, she could not open the front door of the apartment. When there was no response after repeated knockings, a couple of residents in the building gathered and broke open the door. When Yashmoti rushed in, she found her daughter lying on the floor. There was blood on her face and on the floor. There were signs of struggle and rape.

Hours later when doctors declared Hetal dead, people started talking about who would do such a monstrous thing to a child. Few eyewitnesses told the Kolkata police that they suspected the security guard—Dhananjoy Chatterjee—who worked in the building and that he was seen in the area in the afternoon when the incident took place. But Dhananjoy was nowhere to be found. A frantic search began but he remained untraceable for weeks. It was only two months later that he was finally arrested.

WHO WAS DHANANJOY AND WHAT HAPPENED ON 5 MARCH?[1]

Dhananjoy Chatterjee was born on 14 August 1965 in Kuludihi, Bankura district of West Bengal. His life in the village was marked by poverty. Growing up, Dhananjoy knew he had to go to the big city to earn money and sustain his family. His parents were old and he was married. He moved to Kolkata and was hired by Security and Investigating Bureau—whose proprietor was Shyam Karmakar—as a security guard. He was allocated Anand Apartment as his posting. During the investigation, it was revealed that on 2 March 1990,

[1] Based on media reports that surfaced after the incident.

Hetal had complained to her mother Yashmoti Parekh that Dhananjoy had been eve-teasing her when she would move past him and had even proposed to her to accompany him for a movie. She had told her mother about this prior to that as well. Yashmoti informed her husband Nagardas Parekh about this on 3 March who, in turn, complained to Shyam Karmakar and requested him to replace the guard.

Shyam Karmakar came to meet Nagardas at his home and upon hearing the matter requested Nagardas to give a written complaint. Once the complaint was made formal, Dhananjoy was transferred to Paras Apartment and a transfer order was apparently sent to him. Bijoy Thapa, a security guard at Paras Apartment, was asked to replace him at Anand Apartment. The transfer was to take effect from 5 March 1990. However, despite the order of transfer Dhananjoy did not report for duty at his new place on the scheduled date. On being questioned during the investigation process on why he did not report to duty, he said that he could not due to a personal difficulty.

Hetal's mother used to visit Laxmi Narayan Mandir around five in the evening daily. On the day of the murder, she left for the temple at approximately 5:20 PM. At about 6:05 PM, when she returned home and was about to take the elevator, she was told by Ramdhan Yadav, the lift operator, that Dhananjoy had gone to her flat in her absence to call his office. She was annoyed as she knew that he had been harassing her daughter. On reaching her apartment, she rang the bell repeatedly but there was no response from the other end. She sensed that something was wrong. She quickly called for help from the neighbours who broke the lock. She entered her home frantically and found the door of her bedroom open. Hetal was lying on the floor—unmoving. Her skirt and blouse had been pulled up and her private parts and breasts were visible. There were patches of blood on her head and face as well as on the floor. There were bloodstains on her hands and vagina too. The clothes she was wearing were bloodstained. Her underwear was torn and was found lying near the entrance of the apartment. She appeared to be unconscious; Yashmoti lifted her by her arms and pulled her daughter towards the door to take her to a doctor immediately. However, a doctor had been summoned by the neighbours. After examining Hetal in the lift itself, he pronounced her dead.

Hetal Parekh's body was taken back to her flat. Her father was informed. He rushed home and called the Bhawanipore Police Station around 9:15 PM. The police arrived and began with the initial investigation. Sub-Inspector Gurupada Som, along with other police personnel, recorded the FIR based on the statement by Yashmoti and began the investigation. Any evidence that was found was preserved for forensic examination and the statements by the eyewitnesses were recorded.

Dhananjoy had been seen going up to the Parekh residence to use the telephone and have a word with the security agency that had employed him. They had later seen the guard walking down the stairs shortly before Hetal's mother returned home. Thereafter, he was not seen in the building. Neither did he turn up for work nor did he collect his wages. He was nowhere to be found after the incident. The police were convinced that he was absconding and this made him the centre of their investigation. A massive search was initiated but it did not yield any results for a long time.

It was only two months later that the search ended. Dhananjoy was found at his village home at Kuludihi, near Chhatna, Bankura. The police arrested him in the early hours of 12 May 1990. He denied all allegations, claiming innocence, but he had no evidence in his defence.

THE TRIAL

There was no eyewitness to the crime committed so the entire case was based on circumstantial evidence—the evidence recovered from Dhananjoy, the fact that he had absconded right after the crime was committed. Dr Dipankar Guha, who had conducted the post-mortem examination, testified that Hetal was subjected to rape before being murdered. As many as 21 injuries were noted by Dr Dipankar Guha on Hetal's body. The motive was accordingly established by the prosecution and the Alipore Sessions Court sentenced Dhananjoy to death on 12 August 1991.[2]

Dhananjoy made an appeal against his conviction to Calcutta High Court. But the appeal was dismissed and the sentence of death was confirmed by the Calcutta High Court on 7 August 1992. When he approached the Supreme Court, the response was the same. The

---

[2] For a detailed report of the trial, see https://indiankanoon.org/doc/1351933/.

apex court stated that the crime was enough to make it belong to the rarest of rare category, crimes warranting a death sentence.

When a case is completely built on circumstantial evidence, not only do the circumstance should fully establish the guilt but also it should be of a conclusive nature, consistent only with the hypothesis of the guilt of the accused. The sole ground on which the circumstances could be justified should be the guilt of the accused. Any evidence or chain of evidence should be in no way consistent with the innocence of the accused. Legally established circumstances, and not merely indignation of the court, must inform a conviction. The seriousness of the crime calls for greater care when it comes to scrutinising the evidence—proof should never be replaced by suspicion. Since the death sentence was confirmed by both the High Court and the Supreme Court, one must consider the circumstances carefully bearing the principle points mentioned.

The Motive

The prosecution cited that there was sufficient evidence on the record to show that Dhananjoy had a motive to commit the alleged crime contrary to what Dhananjoy's lawyer Mr Ganguli claimed. Hetal used to be teased by Dhananjoy which led to her family requesting for a replacement of Dhananjoy. Dhannajoy's visit to Anand Apartment when he had been transferred to Paras Apartment also raised suspicion. During the cross-examination, the supervisor of Security and

Investigating Bureau—Pratap Chandra Pali—revealed that he had asked the new guard Dasarath Murmu about this as well. Pali had visited Anand Apartment at about 5:45 PM on the day of the incident. When Pali demanded an explanation, Dhananjoy told him that it was on account of 'certain personal inconvenience' that he did not report to duty that day.

Dhananjoy's actions did not seem innocent. His behaviour towards Hetal and the possible motive of revenge for the complaint made against him by Hetal's father pointed towards his guilt.

The Evidence

A number of items were recovered from Dhananjoy's house in the city. The police had gathered from the eyewitness account that he was wearing a cream-coloured shirt and grey trousers when he had gone to her apartment. A cream-coloured button was found in the bedroom where Hetal was found. When he was arrested on 12 May 1990, a cream-coloured shirt and a pant, which he had wrapped in a newspaper, was seized from him.

Forensic examination—as testified by Pratha Sinha, Senior Scientific Officer, Physics Division, Forensic Science Laboratory—revealed that the button found at the crime scene was from the shirt recovered from Dhananjoy's house. The shirt had all the buttons stitched, except for the third button from the top which was of light cream colour, meaning that the button was stitched on later.

A broken chain was also found at the Parekh residence. This chain was traced back to Dhananjoy. Gauranga Chandra, a witness, testified that he had given the chain to Dhananjoy a month before Hetal's murder.

All evidences strongly pointed to his presence in Hetal's room on the day of the murder.

But Why Did Dhananjoy Disappear?

Dhananjoy had no satisfactory explanation to this question, which was raised repeatedly. He stated that he had left Anand Apartment after 2:00 PM to see a movie at a theatre and had then gone to Manorma School to collect his belongings. Then, after buying some fruits he had left for his village to attend the sacred thread ceremony of his younger brother. But he could not produce any evidence or alibi to validate this sequence of events. Dhananjoy's disappearance right after the murder was seen as material evidence which strengthened the prosecution's case.

The Verdict

The rape and murder of Hetal Parekh had shaken society's faith on security due to which the crime was moved to the 'rarest of rare category'. The Supreme Court of India upheld the High Court order and confirmed his act as heinous and sentenced him to death on 11 January 1994. A few days later, on 20 January 1994, the apex court dismissed Dhananjoy's review petition. After this, the only way he could escape the death sentence was by filing a mercy petition to the governor of West Bengal, which he did on 2 February 1994. The governor declared that he would not interfere in the matter and rejected his petition. The next day, Dhananjoy sent a mercy petition to the president of India. He was able to obtain a stay on his execution from the Calcutta High Court because his mercy petition had not been reviewed. His petition was rejected by the president on 23 June 1994 and his execution remained indefinitely deferred.[3]

Meanwhile, a writ petition[4] was filed against the governor's dismissal of Dhananjoy's mercy petition in the Calcutta High Court. The writ petition was dismissed on 14 November 2004, almost a decade later. Dhananjoy Chatterjee again filed a writ petition this time in the High court which again got dismissed on 8 January 2004. Dhananjoy filed few more mercy petitions which got rejected in May 2004 and August 2004, respectively. Since there was no limit to the number of writ petitions that could be filed, he could file more of them and delay his sentence. The repeated delay in carrying out the sentence was being questioned by the public. On 25 June 2004, the opinion of the West Bengal government was sought by the president. Chief Minister Buddhadeb Bhattacharjee said that he fully supported the death sentence. The home ministry too supported the death sentence and the date was finally set.

---

3 For a timeline of the petitions filed by Dhananjoy, see https://www.rediff.com/news/2004/aug/04dhan.htm.

4 A writ petition can be filed in the High Court (Article 226) or the Supreme Court (Article 32) of India when any of your fundamental rights are violated. The jurisdiction with the High Courts (Article 226) with regards to a writ petition is wider and extends to constitutional rights too.

DAYS LEADING TO THE EXECUTION

Dhananjoy had been incarcerated at Alipore Central Jail for over 14 years by this time. When the president had rejected his mercy petition it was a damning blow. His parents and wife had been protesting in the streets of Kolkata against the death sentence but there was a counter-protest too, demanding justice for Hetal. In the days that followed, he listened to bhajans and devotional songs. He spent his last few days reading aloud excerpts from the Bhagavad Gita.

On his last day, he took a bath and sat down to read the Gita for one last time. He then stood up and walked toward the gallows. Eighty-three-year-old Nata Mullick, the chosen hangman, was waiting for Dhananjoy. This was the last hanging of his life. He had conducted 24 hangings in his lifetime and was now set to retire. Nata Mullick was apparently overwhelmed by the cool of Dhananjoy as he offered no resistance and even blessed the hangman but went on claiming his innocence till the last.

'Dhananjoy kept saying, *"Ami Nirdosh. Amake mere phelchhe sab* (I am innocent. They all are killing me) as we led him to the gallows,' Mullick said.

Dhananjoy Chatterjee was hanged at 4:30 AM on 14 August 2004. His last wish was to donate his eyes and kidneys to poor patients.

9

Ajmal Kasab

THE MUMBAI ATTACKS, 2008

On the evening of 26 November 2008, 10 terrorists landed on Mumbai's coast on a rubber dinghy. They had set sail from Karachi in Pakistan where they had been trained in urban warfare by the terrorist outfit Lashkar-e-Taiba (LeT). On landing, the group—all armed with automatic rifles and hand grenades—split into different directions. One group headed towards Taj Mahal Palace in south Mumbai. Another went to Chabbad House while two teams headed towards the Trident and Oberoi hotels in Nariman Point.

The last group, a two-member team, which included Ajmal Kasab, targeted the iconic Chhatrapati Shivaji Maharaj Terminus (CST) railway station.

What followed that evening and for the next three days scarred the nation forever. A crazed killing spree ensued, executed by Kasab and his nine fellow terrorists which left 166 people dead and 238 injured. The dead included 18 policemen and other security personnel and 26 foreign nationals. The loss of property resulting from the terrorist attack was calculated to be over Rs 150 crores. The two luxury hotels and the Jewish synagogue were completely gutted.[1] India was glued to their TV sets while Mumbai was under siege. When the attack finally ended, nine terrorists had been killed and Ajmal Kasab was the only man captured alive.

Kasab's image as the slightly shadowy figure in cargo pants, a fake Versace t-shirt and a rucksack with the cocky swagger of a young man out for the evening was shared across the country. In the image captured by a local photographer, he is seen to be carrying an AK-47. Ajmal Amir Kasab, just 21 years old, had left the country stunned with the horrific and bloody acts that he had carried out with his fellow terrorists.

The United States Department of Defense (DoD) defines terrorism as 'the calculated use of unlawful violence or threat of unlawful violence to inculcate fear; intended to coerce or to intimidate governments or societies in the pursuit of goals that are generally political, religious, or ideological'.[2] The 2008 Mumbai attacks stands as one of the most significant terrorist attacks that India has ever suffered. To borrow from DoD, the attack comprised three key elements—violence, fear and intimidation—meant to attack and subdue the state of India.

WHO WAS AJMAL KASAB?

Mohammed Ajmal Amir Kasab was born on 13 July 1987 to Amir Shahban Kasab and Noor-e-Elahi. The couple belonged to the Qassab community and lived

---

1 https://www.indiatoday.in/india/story/ajmal-kasab-amitabh-bachchan-raw-mumbai-attacks-ramesh-mahale-1396531-2018-11-26

2 https://sites.ualberta.ca/~hsmun/Safeguarding%20human%20rights%20in%20prosecuting%20counter[1].pdf

in the village of Faridkot in Okara district of Pakistan's Punjab. The senior Kasab ran a small snack cart to support the family of five children and his wife. The Kasabs were poor—their elder son Afzal worked as a labourer in Lahore and their elder daughter, Rukaiyya Husain, was married off at an early age and lived in the village. Ajmal was their third child. A younger sister, Suraiyya, and brother, Munir, lived in Faridkot with their parents. Kasab was fond of watching TV and Hindi movies. He was in the habit of chewing tobacco. He was good friends with the village doctor, Mazhar, who had a dispensary near Faridkot bus stop.

After dropping out of school in the year 2000, Kasab and his friend Dittu started working as labourers in Faridkot. In 2001, he and his father went to Lahore in search of employment. In Lahore he lived with his father and uncle, Ghulam Rasool, in a house they rented from Haji Qamar. On his father's instructions, Kasab started working as a labourer at 'Mazdooron Ka Adda'. He worked there for about five years. However, he could not adjust to the tough working environment for long and returned to Faridkot. In 2005, during Eid-al-Fitr, the festival of the breaking of the fast, the family offered prayers like every other year. Ajmal's mother would prepare *sevaiyan* for family. On this occasion, Ajmal asked his father for new clothes; however, his father was not in a position to grant him his wish and hence denied the request. Ajmal got very upset. He could not accept that his father had refused him the simple wish of wearing new clothes. He fought with his father and then the unimaginable happened—an angry Ajmal left home, leaving behind his entire family for ever. He started living at Ali Hajveri Dargah in Lahore. Kasab's friend Shafique got him a job in Welcome Tent Service. Here, the owner of the establishment used to call him 'Balka'. It was here that Kasab met and befriended Muzaffar Lal Khan, who also worked there.

In the next one year, Ajmal would commit petty crimes for money in order to survive. He was a part of an armed robbery too, carried out with the support of his friend Muzaffar. One day, in Rawalpindi, Kasab and Muzaffar were attempting to buy weapons when they encountered members of Jama'at-ud-Da'wah—the political wing of LeT—distributing pamphlets. Ajmal read a pamphlet and was intrigued by the description of a training that was announced. Both of them decided to participate in this training and immediately signed up for it. This decision led them to a remote LeT camp in the mountainous region of Muzaffarabad in Pakistan's Azad Kashmir. This was the base camp, where in the weeks to come, Daura-e-Suffa training lasted 21 days. There were 30 other boys, apart from Kasab and his friend, doing the training. During this, they were first converted from Sunni (sect of Islam) to Ahl-e-Hadis and were given lessons in the Hadis (a study of the things said by the Prophet Muhammad and descriptions of his daily life). An ustad conducted physical exercises. Besides, they were given lectures and lessons on Jihad. He received training in marine warfare from the dreaded LeT.

The second training session lasted for 21 days, they practiced running and climbing over mountains. They were also given training in dismantling and assembling *kalashan*(AK 47 rifles), rifles and pistols and taught how to fire these weapons.

They were given lessons in *hadis,* namaz and the Quran. They were taught to operate rocket launchers and the use of hand grenades. They were also given training in the use of satellite phones, GPS systems and map-reading. The physical exercise comprised staying without food for 60 hours while climbing mountains with heavy loads on the back. Now they were turned into solid 'Jihadis'.

After the completion of the training his 'Ustad' Muavia gave him one thousand and three hundred rupees and asked him to go home and then to Ameer Hafiz Sayeed's the trainer office at Baitul Mujahdin.

In September 2008, they all sailed to the sea at Karachi on two small boats. Here, they were put on a boat with an engine attached to it. On that boat a person called Hakim Saab gave them three days' advance marine training. During the marine training they were taught to read and use maps, to fathom the depths of the sea, to use GPS for marine-ways, to cast fishing nets and to sail in order to deceive the naval officers of the enemy they would say they were fishermen.

Three days later, Abu Hamza, the training-in-charge told them there were more men who had been training like them and they were also going with them to carry out the attack on Hindustan.

On the thirteenth Roza[3], they were called to the office in Baitul Mujahidin. Ameer Hafiz said that the time for

[3] 13th day of Ramzan.

jihad had come and they were now required to consider how best to launch the attack on Hindustan. They said that the economic strength of Hindustan lay in Mumbai and therefore, it was necessary to attack Mumbai. Their marine training was to be used to reach the location by sea.

They were divided into 10 'Mujahedeens' and grouped into 5 *buddiyas* (pairs). The *buddiyas* were: 1. Kasab and Ismail Khan; 2. Imran Babar and Nasir; 3. Soheb and Nazir Ahmed; 4. Hafiz Arshad alias Hayaji and Javed; and 5. Abdul Rehman (Chhota) and Fahadullah.

They were told to carry out a fedayeen[4] attack on the twenty-seventh Roza. For going from Karachi to Mumbai, a Hindustani boat would have to be hijacked. The *maali halat* (financial condition) of Hindustan was based on *videshi sailaniyon* (foreign salesmen). Therefore, in order to weaken the *maali halat* of Hindustan it was necessary to attack, among other places, those places frequented by *videshi sailaniyon*.

26 NOVEMBER 2008

It was any other day for the people of Mumbai. As the sun set, a few local fishermen at Colaba, a seaside promenade, were retiring for the day. They were packing up their things and were about to head home. It was around 9:00 PM when they noticed 10 men in a speedboat coming ashore. Kasab was one among them. The fishermen asked the men who they were? Kasab told

[4] Fedayeen is a term used to refer to various military groups willing to sacrifice themselves for a cause.

them that they were students. Ismail had an altercation with them. Other disappeared into the darkness, except Fahadullah and Abdul Rehman (Chhota) who started the boat and set off to some other place.

On the way, Ismail said to them that first he and Kasab would leave for VTS by taxi, then Soheb and Nazir Ahmad would go to Leopold Hotel by taxi, and then Javed and Hafiz Arshad would go to the Taj Hotel by taxi. Imran Babar and Nasir would walk to Nariman House. Last of all, Fahadullah and Abdul Rehman (Chhota) would go to Oberoi Hotel in the speedboat. Ismail asked Kasab, Soheb and Javed to place RDX bombs, under their taxi drivers' seats.

Chhatrapati Shivaji Terminus (CST)
9:30 PM

Mumbai's historic railway terminus was teeming with people, most returning home after the day's work. Amidst the noise and commotion, Kasab and his friend Ismail Khan, slipped in without being noticed. Suddenly, there was a noise of rapid gunshots and before people could even process what was actually happening, bodies were falling to the ground. People ran to save their lives, frantic and desperate. They ran over the dead bodies and some slipped on the blood on the floor. A few people lost their lives to in the panic that was created.

Kasab had achieved what he had been told to do.

Maharashtra Anti-Terrorism Squad (ATS) Chief Hemant Karkare was at his residence in Dadar around 9:45 PM. He received important information about a attack at CST. The bad news was that it was not only CST which was under attack but it appeared that there was were simultaneous attacks on several high-profile locations in Mumbai, including Nariman House, Leopold Café at Colaba Causeway , Taj Hotel at the Gateway of India and the Oberoi Trident at Nariman Point. Karkare knew that they had to act immediately to contain whatever this was. He wasted no time and immediately left his home and proceeded towards CST with his team. The team included encounter specialist Vijay Salaskar, Additional Commissioner of Mumbai Police Ashok Kamte and four constables.

Cama Hospital
10:30 PM

Kasab and Ismail ended their assault around 10:00 PM—an attack which led to the death of 58 people.[5] Their objective having been completed, they left the field of attack.

The police continued to fire at them and tried to stop them. Ismail and Kasab shot the policemen dead and came out of VT station through the stairs. After coming down from the overbridge, they looked for a taxi in the lane (Badruddin Tayabji Marg). Since they didn't find any, they moved ahead in the lane and started firing. The police responded with heavy firing so they decided to enter the opposite building (which happened to be Cama Hospital). After climbing to the terrace, they fired at the policemen and threw grenades at them, killing them in the process.

5 https://www.indiatoday.in/india/story/how-2611-mumbai-terror-attack-happened-in-2008-from-first-eyewitness-to-kasab-1094473-2017-11-26

When they realised that the building they had entered was a hospital, they decided to check the rooms and fired at the people they found. But all the doors were closed from inside and the iron-grill doors provided additional protection. Unable to open any of the doors, the duo decided to exit the hospital. They came down and moved forward taking cover behind a wall. Eventually they jumped over the wall and came out on to the road.

That was when they saw a car, with its headlights on, coming towards them from the opposite direction. Once the car was near enough, they fired at it and at the same time shots were fired from the car. Kasab had been hit on both his hands. When the firing from the car stopped, they looked inside the car and found that all the policemen inside were dead. They tried to open the car's rear door but it did not open. An injured Kasab leant against the vehicle. His hands were shaking while Ismail then went to the front of the car and pulled out the dead bodies of the driver and the policeman sitting behind the driver. Then Kasab pulled out the dead body of the policeman sitting next to the driver and threw it on the ground. There were no rounds left in Ismail's *kalashan* and, therefore, he picked up the policeman's *kalashan* from the car. He started the car and drove at full speed. It was at this point that he revealed to Kasab that bullets had hit him on the legs and in the armpits.

After some time it appeared that the back right tyre of their car was punctured. In spite of that Ismail continued to drive the car at a very high speed. Then, on seeing a white car approaching from the opposite direction, Ismail stopped their car. Kasab fired from his *kalashan* in the air and both of them got out of the car. He went towards the white car and, pointing the *kalashan* at the driver, asked him to stop the car. The driver immediately stopped the car. Ismail pulled him out. At the same time the person sitting next to the driver and the woman sitting on the back seat also got out. All this while, Kasab was covering Ismail. Having thus snatched the car, Ismail sat on the driver's seat and Kasab quickly sat next to him and they left. At this point Kasab asked Ismail where should they go next. Ismail said they had to go to Malabar Hill.

As they drove on, they came across the barricade on the road manned by policemen. The policemen had seen their car moving at great speed from a long distance and were asking them to stop by raising their hands and blowing their whistles. Realizing that it was impossible to cross the barricade by smashing against it, Kasab asked Ismail to stop the car at some distance from the barricade and to keep the headlights on so that the policemen would not be able to see either them or the number of their car. Ismail did as he was told. The policemen were shouting at them and asking them to switch off the headlights.

Realising the gravity of the situation they both raised their hands. But the policemen kept coming at them. Ismail tried to pick up the *kalashan* but was not able to reach it as it was kept under the seat. He then picked up his pistol, which was kept on the seat, and fired at the policemen. At the same time, Kasab saw a policeman coming towards him, he opened the door of the car and got hold of his *kalashan*. The police had started firing. A policeman tried to snatch the *kalashan* from Kasab. In the struggle, Kasab fell down but he had his finger on the trigger and he pressed it. The bullets hit a policeman he collapsed on the ground. The other policemen beat Kasab with lathis and snatched the *kalashan* from his hands. Ismail was injured in the police firing and soon succumbed to his injuries.

There was silence for the next few minutes. The police force slowly moved towards the vehicle. While his companion lay dead, Kasab pretended to be dead too, lying motionless in his seat. Assistant Sub-Inspector Tukaram Omble inched close towards the car. A ferociously courageous man, though unarmed went on to open the door of the car and immediately realised that Kasab was alive. Within a split of a second, Kasab had aimed his gun at the police but Omble held on to the barrel of his rifle, enabling other officers to apprehend him. All this while, Kasab fired several shots. But the police officers managed to accomplish what they had intended to do but this succes came with a heavy price. Omble had taken over 20 bullets from an AK-47 at point-blank range and did not survive. Another brave man and a valiant officer of the Mumbai Police lost his life in the struggle to capture Kasab.

CONFESSIONS AND TRIALS

The arrest of Ajmal Kasab, the only terrorist captured alive after the 26/11 attack ended, created a huge media and public furore. Interrogators wanted to record his statement on video; however, Kasab insisted on turning off the camera and said that he wouldn't speak unless it had been done. Nonetheless, the following confessions were recorded on camera. A number of crucial details revealed by him helped the investigators create a timeline. He disclosed to them how he and his team had entered India via the sea and captured hijacked an Indian trawler to enter Mumbai's coastal waters. They were provided with a satellite phone and a global positioning device to help them navigate while at sea. Kasab told the police that he and his friend, Ismail Khan, were the ones who shot ATS Chief Hemant Karkare, Encounter Specialist Vijay Salaskar and Additional Commissioner Ashok Kamte. Later, a great deal of information regarding his origin, nationality, and his involvement in the entire 26/11 attacks were recorded.

When Kasab's case went to trial, the question that arose was who would represent him to ensure a fair trial. No lawyers stepped forward to defend him. The Esplanade Court Bar Association even passed a resolution that none of them would defend Ajmal. Shiv Sena activists also threatened any lawyer from taking up his case. Not giving Kasab a lawyer would have been equivalent to denying him a fair trial which would have reflected poorly on India, so the Bombay High Court intervened. Advocate Anjali Waghmare accepted the nomination to represent him, but she was removed on 15 April 2009. After her Advocate Abbas Kazmi was appointed as the defence counsel. He too was removed from the case on 30 November and was replaced by Advocate KP Pawar.[6]

---

[6] For the timeline of the case, please see https://www.thehindu.com/news/national/Ajmal-Kasab-trial-%E2%80%93-Timeline/article12515678.ece

On 3 May 2010, Kasab was found guilty of 80 offences, including murder, waging war against India, possessing explosives, and other charges. On 6 May 2010, the same trial court sentenced him to death on four counts and life imprisonment on five counts.

Special Court Justice ML Tahaliyani condemned the attack and its perpetrators as 'no ordinary criminals' and the attack as 'an act of war', while public prosecutor Ujjwal Nikam referred to Kasab as 'exceptionally depraved and a killing machine bereft of human nature'.[7]

Kasab appealed to the Bombay High Court to avoid a death penalty. The two lawyers—Amin Solkar and Farhana Shah—were tasked with defending Kasab, after they were nominated by then acting Chief Justice of Bombay High Court J N Patel. Solkar and Shah had argued for Kasab in the Bombay High Court against his death sentence almost on a day-to-day basis for nearly nine months. The bench, which comprised Justice Ranjanaa Desai and Justice Ranjit More, upheld the verdict of the trial court on 21 February 2011. He further challenged his conviction at the Supreme Curt of India on 30 July 2011. The Bombay High Court's orders were stayed as his case was heard in the apex court. On 29 August 2012, a bench composed of Justice Aftab Alam and Justice Chandramouli Kumar Prasad found him guilty and sentenced him to death yet again.

---

[7] https://www.indiatoday.in/magazine/india-today-archives/story/20100517-the-inside-story-742884-2010-05-07

HONOURING THE BRAVEHEARTS

While Kasab's case went to trail in court and the nation awaited justice, the valiant heroes who jumped into action during the attacks were honoured by the government of India. Hemant Karkare, Vijay Salaskar and Ashok Kamte were honoured with the Ashok Chakra, the country's highest peacetime gallantry award, for their patriotism, bravery and fearlessness on 26 January 2009. Major Sandeep Unnikrishnan, Special Action Group of the National Security Guard (NSG), who fought and was martyred during the Taj Palace attack, was also honoured with the Ashok Chakra for his bravery, leadership and sacrifice for the nation. Tukaram Omble, whose final act of selflessness had led to the capture of Kasab, was honoured with the Ashok Chakra for his act of daring, fearlessness and self-sacrifice.

The martyrs were honoured by the nation while the culprit still awaited his punishment.

THE ROAD TO PUNISHMENT

By 5 November 2012, when President Pranab Mukherjee rejected Kasab's mercy petition, four years had passed since that terrible incident in the city of Mumbai. Two days later, on 7 November, Union Minister of Home Affairs Sushil Kumar Shinde confirmed the rejection of the mercy plea. The order papers were sent to the Maharashtra government on 8 November. On 10 November, the Ministry of Home Affairs and the Maharashtra government declared that Kasab will be hanged on 21 November 2012. The entire sequence of events moved fast and efficiently and was kept a secret from the public. The death and funeral of Shiv Sena patriarch Bal Thackeray also helped in diverting attention

Meanwhile, Kasab was moved from Mumbai's Arthur Road Jail to Yerwada Central Jail in Pune. Apart from the jail superintendent, nobody in Yerwada was made aware of who was brought in from Mumbai. Kasab was kept in a special cell. Throughout the period of incarceration, Kasab had hopes that he would somehow escape the death penalty. However, when the presidential mercy didn't come through, it was a heavy blow. An officer of the Arthur Road Jail stated later, 'In fact ever since his appeal had been rejected by the Supreme Court, his attitude was that of resignation. He knew that his death was a foregone conclusion and it was a matter of time and did not even react much when we informed him that his mercy petition had been rejected by the president. Hence towards the end, he did not emote much or display any remorse.'[8]

The morning of 21 November 2012 finally arrived. Kasab had barely slept the night before. The jail officials had told him to wake up at 4:00 AM. When he was asked whether he would like to eat anything specifically, Kasab said that he wanted to eat tomatoes; so he was given a basketful to have a last taste. Kasab's last wish was to meet his family but despite informing the Pakistani government about his execution, they had failed to respond.

---

[8] https://web.archive.org/web/20121127172052/http://www.hindustantimes.com/India-news/Mumbai/Last-words-Dobara-aisi-galti-nahi-karunga/Article1-962444.aspx

At 7:20 AM, Kasab was finally brought to the gallows. It was only a few minutes before Kasab's execution that the executioner was informed whom he would be hanging. In attendance too was a special magistrate, a district administration official, a doctor, a medical team and a few jail officials. Dressed in the jail uniform, his hands and legs were tied. It would be the last time when Kasab would see the light of the day. Finally, a black cloth was covered on his head and the noose placed around his neck. The executioner pulled the lever at 7:30 AM. Later, Home Minister Shinde confirmed the time of death of Ajmal Kasab to the nation.

THE END OF THE ROAD

Kasab had been executed secretly and buried at Punes's Yerwada prison. After his execution was revealed to the world, the Pakistani Taliban threatened revenge unless Kasab's body was returned to his family. 'If his body is not given to us or his family, we will, God willing, carry on his mission,' Ahsan told The Associated Press by telephone from an undisclosed location. 'We will take revenge for his murder.'[9]

In India, the news of Kasab's death was a moment of closure and relief. Justice had arrived although very late. While Uttar Pradesh banned any celebrations and public gatherings, the Coimbatore police department took a couple of people in preventive custody for celebrating Kasab's execution. Many felt that this was a fitting response to all the terrorist organisations and

---

[9] https://www.theguardian.com/world/2012/nov/22/pakistani-taliban-demand-mumbai-terrorist

would deter any future attacks.[10] But there were quite a few who believed that Kasab was merely a foot soldier whose execution was not the answer to terror as many of the masterminds were still safe and alive. For them justice had still not been done.[11]

Indian External Affairs Minister Salman Khurshid announced on the same day that the Indian government would respect any request made by the Pakistani government and Kasab's family to hand over his body. It was unlikely that Pakistan would ever accept Kasab's body, given that it was only in January 2009 after much pressure on part of the India that he was recognised as a Pakistani citizen by Pakistan. Since there was no such request made, Kasab still remains buried in Indian soil.

[10] https://www.washingtonpost.com/news/worldviews/wp/2012/11/21/how-india-reacted-to-mumbai-gunman-ajmal-kasabs-execution/?utm_term=.070ebbd98dfd

[11] https://www.livemint.com/Opinion/b4mEzysUGZ8KiqZOf5fz1M/Ajmal-Kasabs-hanging-death-of-an-ignorant-footsoldier.html

10

Afzal Guru

13 DECEMBER 2001

Parliament House, New Delhi

That morning, at 11:30 AM, it was foggy and the capital was shivering. The Indian Parliament was in its winter session. It had been 40 minutes since both Rajya Sabha and Lok Sabha sessions had been adjourned for the day. The prime minister, Atal Bihari Vajpayee, and the leader of the opposition, Sonia Gandhi, had left some time back. There were, however, around a hundred members of Parliament (MPs), including Home Minister LK Advani and Minister of State for Defence Harin Pathak, in the premises.

The Parliament House Building is a circular building having 12 entry points through huge wooden gates numbered 1 to 12 in the anti-clockwise direction. Wooden gate No. 11 is for the entry and exit of the Vice-President to the Parliament House and other wooden gates are used by different designated officials for entry and exit in the Parliament House Building. Encircling the building of the Parliament House is a circular road. The circular road has open areas abutting it. Seven entrances from the roads outside lead into the complex, down the passage, ending at the circular road. At each entrance, there is an iron gate. These gates are numbered as iron gate Nos. 1 to 7 in the anti-clockwise direction. Iron gate Nos. 1 and 2 are towards the Southern and Northern side respectively of the entry to Parliament House Complex through Sansad Marg. Iron gate Nos. 3 and 4 are at the entry points to the Complex from Lok Sabha Marg. Iron gate Nos. 5 and 7 are at the entry points to the Complex from Rajya Sabha Marg and iron gate No. 6 is at the T-Junction entry point to the Complex on the Rajya Sabha Marg.

Fresh from his training at the Central Reserve Police Force's (CRPF) academy at Neemaj, Constable Santosh was part of the 23rd Battalion, guarding the Parliament House, at Gate Number 6—the 'Iron Gate', the T-Junction entry point to the Complex on the Rajya Sabha Marg. Around 11:40 AM, he heard sounds of firing and sensed trouble. Before he could conclude anything, there was a huge explosion. A gun battle ensued as security personnel returned fire and one of the intruders detonated explosives strapped to his waist. The attack killed 14 people, including police and security personnel, a gardener, a journalist and the terrorists themselves.

India was stunned by the audacity of the attack.

IN THE VALLEY OF KASHMIR

Kashmir, the northernmost region of the Indian subcontinent, the valley lying between the Great Himalayas and the Pir Panjal range, is paradise on earth Sadly, conflicts and insurgency has ravaged this paradise in the recent decades. Suyyapur, also known as Sopore, is a town in the Baramulla district of Jammu and Kashmir. Habibullah and his wife Ayesha Begum lived in Du Aabgah, a village near Sopore. Habibullah ran a timber and transport business to support his family. By the end of June 1969, summer was halfway through, and Ayesha Begum was about to deliver a child. On 30 June 1969, Ayesha went into labour. It was a tense moment for the soon-to-be father, Habibullah, but the delivery was smooth and Ayesha gave birth to a baby boy. The couple named him Afzal Guru.

Afzal's childhood could almost be called idyllic. He grew up in a kingdom of green and blue—rice fields, meadows, trees and lakes. However, tragedy struck early. Habibullah passed away by chronic liver cirrhosis when Afzal was still only 12 and the mother and son were left to fend for themselves. Afzal joined a government school in Sopore and successfully completed his schooling in 1988. He wished to pursue higher education and took admission in Jhelum Valley Medical College to pursue an MBBS degree. He had a smooth sailing through his first year but fate had something else in store for him. As thousands of Kashmiris crossed Line of Control (LoC) for arms training in 1989, Afzal followed the trend and left his medical degree halfway and crossed over to the other side of Kashmir, but in a matter of weeks got disillusioned and came back and tried to live a normal life. Afzal returned to India and ran a small business of his own in Sopore, Kashmir. He worked as a commission agent in fruits trade in Anantnag, the trading centre of Kashmir Valley. Afzal's business venture brought him into contact with a man named Tariq of Anantanag, who motivated him to join 'Jihad' for the liberation of Kashmir and assured him of financial assistance. Tariq introduced him to one Gazi Baba (proclaimed offender) in Kashmir.

In 1990, at the peak of the insurgency that claimed a generation of young men in Kashmir, Afzal crossed over the Line of Control once again and headed to Muzaffarabad, Pakistan-occupied Kashmir to be trained as a militant. He became a member of the Jammu Kashmir Liberation Front (JKLF), a political organisation in Jammu & Kashmir founded by Amanullah Khan and Maqbool Bhat. Originally a militant wing of the Plebiscite Front, it changed its name to JKLF in Birmingham, England on 29 May 1977. It was an active militant organisation until 1994. After being initiated into the organisation, he returned to his hometown, where he led around 300 rebels on the same path he was traversing. He would continue to actively work as a militant leader until 1996 when his family advised him to leave this life behind. By then he too, like many others, had been greatly disillusioned by the fact that both India and Pakistan were using the Kashmiri youth as pawns for political gains. He decided to heed to the advice of his family and surrendered to the Border Security Force.

Thereafter, he returned to Delhi where he worked as an area manager in a pharmaceutical firm. He was also a commission agent for medical and surgical goods. As a part of his job, he used to shuttle between the two cities, Delhi and Srinagar. In 1998, he got married to Tabasum Guru. It seemed as if his life had finally fallen into place after all the ups and downs. But it was not to be.

In an interview, while in jail, Afzal shared: "Two days after my marriage, I was picked up by one Maj. Thapa of the Rashtriya Rifles; later Maj. Raj Mohan also called me and they tortured me and gave electric shock to my private parts. Many times I was made to clean their toilets and sweep their camps. Once I had to bribe the security men with all that I had to escape from the Humhama STF torture camp. D.S.P. Vinay Gupta and D.S.P. Davinder Singh supervised the torture. One of their torture experts, Inspector Shanty Singh, electrified me for three hours until I agreed to pay one lakh rupees as bribe. My wife sold her jewelry and for the remaining amount they sold my scooter. I left the camp broken both financially and mentally.[1]

12 DECEMBER 2001

Beyond the Valley

When Afzal Guru was in Pakistan, he was motivated for jihad. There, he was trained in arms. He was also educated on missions to carry out attacks on institutions like Parliament and embassies by the Jaish-e-Mohammed (JeM) leader himself. Then, after returning to India, Guru continued with the activities that he was taught. He took other rebels along with him for the liberation of Kashmir. His experience with the militants and torture at the hands of the security forces of India pushed him back into the world that he had tried to leave behind him. He used to discuss this with his cousin Shaukat Hussain Guru for long hours and SAR Gilani, a lecturer of Arabic at Delhi University. Both Shaukat and Gilani

[1] https://shaheedafzalguru.wordpress.com/story-in-brief/

would be arrested along with Afzal for the attack on the Parliament.

On the cold night of 12 December 2001, Afzal Guru was in Delhi with Mohammad, one of the alleged members of the JeM, with Shaukat and Gilani. Five Pakistani terrorists who would unleash terror in the capital the next day visited them at their hideout. Mohammad took the lead and explained to them in detail about the plan that was to be executed the following day. They were given 10 lakh rupees and a laptop which was used to create fake Home Ministry passes and identity cards. The plan to attack the Parliament had been in the works for a long time now. Guru had provided shelter to the militants, as well as the car which would take them to their destination. His house was also used to store explosives. When the sun rose above the horizon, India would have a new story to read in front of them.

13 DECEMBER 2001

Outside the Parliament

The terrorists waited by the Parliament in the car. They were armed with rifles, grenade launchers, pistols and grenades. Fake identity cards and passes allowed them to gain entry inside the premises. At about 11:35 AM, a white Ambassador car issued by the Home Ministry drove towards the carcade of the vice president. ASI Jeet Ram, the security personnel escorting the vice president of India in a white Ambassador car, was blocking the way, so the gunmen turned their car turned left. ASI Jeet Ram asked them to stop the car but the driver reversed and while doing so, struck the car of the vice president.

ASI Ram and Shekher, the driver of the car of the vice president, managed to stop the car and caught the collar of the terrorist behind the wheel. The driver's actions made ASI Ram suspect that something was wrong, so he took out his revolver. As the five men got out of the car, he fired at one of them. The terrorists were soon in panic and fired back. One of the bullets hit ASI Ram's right thigh. This gave the terrorists enough time to flee.

Constable Kamlesh Kumari of the CRPF was the first to spot the terrorists. She acted according to protocol and raised alarm in order to alert the other security personnel. Her quick thinking brought them to the scene but she lost her life as the terrorists fired at her. The vice president's guards and security personnel shot back at the terrorists and immediately closed the gates of the compound. The terrorists were now trapped.

When cornered by the security personnel, one of the terrorists detonated a human bomb, causing a huge explosion. The other terrorists who had their eyes set on the entry wall looked for an entrance in the ensuing chaos. Constable Kumar and Senior Inspector Mohan Prakash wasted no time and strategically positioned themselves behind a tree. They checked and loaded their weapons, all set to confront the terrorists. At 11:40 AM Inspector Santokh Singh who was stationed at iron gate No. 5, heard the gunshots and alerted his force. They took their positions at building gate No. 5. Inspector Singh saw four persons in military uniforms with *pithoo* bags on their back, running towards wooden gate No. 5 as wooden gate No. 9 had been closed by that time. There was an exchange of fire between the force led by him and the four gunmen. While three of them were killed in the firing, one succeeded in running towards wooden gate No. 5. The lone terrorist started throwing grenades and the men led by Inspector Singh retaliated with bullets. Soon enough the bullets hit their mark and the last of the terrorists was killed.

During the exchange of fire between the intruders and the security forces that day, eight security personnel and one CPWD gardener were martyred. Among the 16 injured, 13 were security personnel.

THE SEARCH FOR THE MASTERMINDS

The attack had been a bold attempt to cripple the Indian government. Apprehending the masterminds and ensuring justice for the victims was of the utmost priority. Having searched the dead thoroughly, call reports of the mobile phones of the terrorists were examined. It came to light that most of the calls they had received were from Dubai and Pakistan.

Inspector Mohan Chand Sharma from the Operation Cell, Lodhi Road, was deputed to investigate the mobile numbers found written on the slips of paper recovered from the terrorists, as also the mobile phones and the three SIM cards recovered from terrorists. The same evening the telecom companies sent back the reports which revealed that two of the numbers were of Essar and were Cash Card numbers. The third was of Airtel, a regular card number of one SAR Gilani who resided in Mukherjee Nagar.

Since the name and address of Gilani had come within the knowledge of the investigating agency, his house was put under surveillance. With no new developments in sight, the surveillance was removed and later remounted 14 December 2001. On the same day, a suspicious phone call was taped. The caller and the receiver were talking to each other in the Kashmiri language. At about 8:00 PM, the same day, another call was taped. This time the conversation was in Hindi and between a man and a woman. When the telecom companies were contacted, it was found that both the calls had originated from Srinagar. The Srinagar Police, Central Agency were alerted.

The next day, Gilani was apprehended on being identified by the landlord and at the time of his arrest, a mobile containing the number traced back to him was seized. He was questioned about the recent phone calls made by him using the mobile. Gilani revealed that he had contacted Afzal and Shaukat, and led the investigating team to Shaukat's house. It was Afsan Guru, Afzal's wife who answered the doorbell. Her mobile was seized as well. She too had been contacted by a number from Srinagar.

Gilani disclosed that he hailed from Baramulla and that Shaukat who was also from Baramulla met him when he was studying for MA. They became friends. About one and a half year ago, Shaukat had introduced him to his cousin Afzal. They used to discuss freedom of Kashmir, Islam and jihad. Shaukat had introduced him to Mohammad, as being associated with JeM and right-hand man of the founder of the terrorist outfit, Masood Azhar and Gazi Baba. He also testified that once the arms had been arranged, five fidayeen members of JeM. being Raja, Rana, Hamja, Hayder and Mohammad had met at the house of Shaukat along with Afzal and Afsan Guru to discuss the plan to attack the Parliament. Afzal had managed to get his hands on a map of the Parliament. Plans to purchase car, explosives and police uniform were discussed. Thereafter, a survey was conducted and the plan was finalised.

Afsan Guru, in her disclosure, revealed that truck no. HR-38E-6733 which Afzal and Shaukat had used to escape to Srinagar was financed by her parents in her name. She disclosed about arranging accommodation for Mohammad at Christian Colony, arranging arms and explosives. Other details regarding the plan to attack the Parliament, including the money and laptop supplied by Mohammad to Shaukat, were also provided by her. Srinagar Police was immediately informed of the latest developments in the case.

Abdul Haq Bhutt, Deputy Superintendent of Police, Srinagar received updates from Delhi on 15 December 2001 in the morning about the Afzal and Shaukat. He formed two to three teams to locate the truck. At about 8:00 AM, he was able to locate the truck in the Fruit Mandi, but as there was a big crowd, they did not disturb the occupants but kept a watch. At about 10:00 AM the truck started from Fruit Mandi and proceeded towards Baramulla and was stopped near Parampura Police Station. Soon Afzal and Shaukat were taken into police custody. After being searched and interrogated, they disclosed that they had Rs 10 lakhs, a computer and a mobile phone with them. Delhi Police was informed about the arrest. At about 2:15 PM they were handed over to the Delhi Police officials who had arrived in Srinagar.

THE TRIAL[2]

By May 2002, a fast track court had started with the proceedings. Afzal Guru was kept in a high-security cell. A large chunk of evidence had been mounted against Guru, especially the mobile and laptop confiscated at the time of his arrest. According to the court, the following circumstances clearly established Guru's association with the terrorists. Guru knew the dead terrorists as he clearly identified their bodies. The call records of his cell phone showed that he was in constant touch with one terrorist killed in the attack, Mohammad. They had talked about other possible locations across Delhi for the attacks. The trial was concluded in nearly six months. After considering the seriousness of the crime and the consequences, justice, according to the court, would only be served if capital punishment were awarded to the offender. Subsequently, Afzal Guru, Gilani, Shaukat Hussain and Afsan Guru were sentenced to death for waging a war against the state.

An appeal was made to the Delhi High Court for Afzal Guru and the other convicts. The Delhi High Court found confirmed Afzal's conviction and after a thorough study of the case and taking into consideration various authorities and precedents, the appeal was dismissed. However, the co-accused in the case, SAR Gilani and Afsan Guru were acquitted on 29 October 2003.

---

[2] For more details, see https://indiankanoon.org/doc/1031426/

Afzal Guru took his case to the Supreme Court, but the apex court upheld the Delhi High Court verdict for Guru, while Shaukat's death sentence was reduced to 10 years of rigorous imprisonment. Guru filed a review petition before the Supreme Court seeking a review of its judgement. The Supreme Court rejected the review petition as well on 22 September 2005. Tabasum Guru, Afzal Guru's wife, filed a mercy petition to the then president of India, APJ Abdul Kalam as a last resort.

Three years later, Shaukat Hussain was released from Tihar Jail, Delhi on account of his good conduct, while Guru still waited for the response to the mercy petition which would decide his fate.

THE VOICES OF OPPOSITION

Guru's trial and conviction, though celebrated by many, was also subjected to criticism on grounds of an unfair trial when the specifics of the same were made public. Arundhati Roy, the Booker Prize-winning author and political activist argued that Guru had been denied natural justice in her book, *The Hanging of Afzal Guru and the Strange Case of the Attack on the Indian Parliament* (2006).[3] Praful Bidwai, a journalist and political activist, was one of the notable personalities who castigated the trial. Former Jammu and Kashmir Chief Minister Mufti Mohammed Sayeed and local political groups voiced their support for clemency for Guru. A number of human rights organisations too voiced their concerns regarding the judgement. Amidst all the

3 https://www.theguardian.com/commentisfree/2013/feb/10/hanging-afzal-guru-india-democracy

opposition and verbal wars, which were not changing the determined outcome, Afzal Guru knew that his end was near.

THE YEAR BEFORE THE HANGING

In November 2012, the Ministry of Home Affairs, headed by the Home Minister Sushil Kumar Shinde, received a handful of cases to be reviewed sent by the president of India. These cases files also included those of Afzal Guru. The Home Minister did not look at the file until the winter session of Parliament was concluded on 20 December 2012. Shinde studied the case file of Guru and recommended a date for the execution—23 January 2013.

His pending petition extended Afzal's by a month, but on 3 February 2013, the President of India Pranab Mukherjee rejected the final mercy petition filed by Guru's wife. A new date was set for the execution—9 February 2013.

OPERATION THREE STAR

Guru's execution was carried out by the government with the utmost secrecy. Afzal Guru's execution was illegal. The government flouted the procedure established by law in executing Afzal Guru the way it did and the Constitution is categorical, in Article 21, that no one shall be deprived of life or personal liberty except according to procedure established by law. The relatives too "shall be informed" about the date of the execution on receipt of final confirmation.

It was reported that Afzal Guru was buried in jail "in accordance with a directive from the Delhi administration, with the jail authorities saying that there was no request from the family to claim it"[4]. This was a deliberate and self-serving distortion of facts. There was no public announcement nor were his family members informed. The government code-named the operation: Operation Three Star.

Afzal Guru had been in solitary confinement for twelve years in Tihar Jail. His last wish was to leave a message for his wife. He wanted to write a letter for her. He requested the jail authorities to try and fulfil his wish. He was provided with a pen and paper to write the letter which was posted to his hometown the same day.

Only a few officials were aware of his scheduled death—absolute confidentiality had been maintained throughout the operation. They were asked to come early Saturday morning. With only a few hours remaining before the scheduled time of hanging, Afzal Guru was calm. He had come to terms with the fact that he stood on the verge of death. He performed his morning prayers and read a few pages of the Quran.

Afzal Guru was hanged on 9 February 2013 at 8:00 AM in Tihar Jail, New Delhi.

---

4 https://economictimes.indiatimes.com/news/politics-and-nation/afzal-guru-government-did-not-intend-to-inform-his-family-in-advance/articleshow/18507531.cms?from=mdr

11

Yakub Memon

On 12 March 1993, multiple blasts across Mumbai sent the city reeling, killing more than 200 people and leaving about 1400 injured. The bombings were metropolitan India's first exposure to terror[1]. There was fire, violent and ferocious, turning everything in its way to ashes. The city was shocked like never before. It saw death continuously ride its chariot for two hours. Though Mumbai faced terrorism many times over after 1993, it has always managed to rise above terror. But it took more than two decades for justice to finally be served to the victims of the 1993 blasts.

LIVING A DOUBLE LIFE

On 30 July 1962, in Mumbai, Abdul Razzak Memon, a former small-time cricketer, and his wife Hanifa happily welcomed their third son, Yakub Abdul Razzak Memon. Tiger Memon, Yakub's eldest brother, only four years older than him, would later play a crucial role in Yakub's life. Yakub, like his brothers, was born and brought up in the Byculla neighbourhood in South

1 https://www.bbc.com/news/world-asia-india-33713846

Mumbai. He had a normal childhood, with regular studies and play. He was enrolled in an English medium school and was on his way to become the most educated member of the Memon family. After completing his schooling, he decided to pursue B.Com. A promising student as he was, he wanted to add one more feather onto his course of education. His vision for the future was crystal clear. He knew where to set his feet exactly. In 1986, Yakub enrolled in the Institute of Chartered Accountants of India. He showed a keen interest in digging deep into the concepts of audit, taxation, finance and general management. He successfully completed his study in four years, becoming a qualified chartered accountant in 1990. His elder brother Tiger had, by this time, already built a reputation for himself in the dark underworld.

In 1991, one year after completing his study of chartered accountancy, Yakub decided to start his own accounting firm. He was confident that he could turn a start-up into an emerging brand. With his childhood friend Chetan Mehta, he started a firm called Mehta and Memon Associates. Chetan both as a friend and a business partner was very supportive to Yakub. However, friendship has its own ways. Sometimes it lasts longer than a lifetime and sometimes ends sooner than we might have expected. After a successful run for about a year, the friends parted ways. Yakub's firm closed down in 1992.

Despite the setback, he was in no mood to give up. Yakub decided to continue from where he had left off. He founded another accountancy firm AR & Sons, naming the second venture after his father. Perhaps his father's name turned out to be a lucky charm for him or maybe it was his own confidence but this firm became very successful. He won the Best Chartered Accountant of the Year award from the Memon community of Mumbai. Yakub had tasted success and he knew that he could recreate it again, so he decided to set up another firm—this time he ventured into export. He founded an export firm, Tejareth International, with its office at Samrat Cooperative Society, Mahim, to export meat to the Middle East. Yakub became financially successful. He invested in six flats in the Al-Hussaini Building in Mahim. Later, he and his entire family shifted to Mahim.

Tiger Memon had chosen a different path. The Babri Masjid at Ayodhya was demolished on 6 December 1992. After its demolition, violence broke out throughout the country. In order to take revenge of the said demolition, Tiger Memon and Dawood Ibrahim, a resident of Dubai, planned to commit a terrorist attack on the city of Bombay. Dawood Ibrahim agreed to send arms and ammunition from abroad. Tiger Memon, in association with his men, particularly, the accused persons, received those arms and ammunition in coastal Bombay. As part of the said conspiracy, Tiger Memon sent some of the accused persons to Dubai and from there to Pakistan for training to handle arms and ammunition.

In the foreground, there was success and fame for Yakub. He had married Raheen in a luxurious ceremony at the Islam Gymkhana. A successful business and a happy marriage, his life seemed to be perfect. But things only seem perfect when looked at from a distance. Only when examined more closely does one see what is hidden underneath.

Tiger Memon had his own underworld empire and Yakub became a part of this world when he started handling Tiger's funds. As per the case files, he funded the training of the 15 young men who were sent to Pakistan to learn arms and ammunition handling. A number of heavy cash transactions under various accounts at the Mahim branch of the Development Cooperative Bank, conducted between December 1992 and March 1993, were later traced back to Tejareth International and Al-Taj Exports. Careful financial planning was underway to fund something big, a nefarious plot that would soon engulf Mumbai in darkness.

A CITY IN ASHES

Established in 1875, the Bombay Stock Exchange (BSE) is located at Dalal Street, Kala Ghoda, Mumbai. The BSE, Asia's first and the world's fastest stock exchange, went into a state of shock on 12 March 1993 at 1:30 PM. An explosion tore through the BSE building leaving everyone shell shocked. This was only the first of twelve bombs that would go off across the city. Other targets included Katha Bazaar, Sena Bhavan, Century Bazaar, Mahim Causeway, Air India Building, Zaveri Bazaar, Hotel Sea Rock, Plaza Theatre, Juhu Centaur Hotel, Airport Bay-54 and Airport Centaur Hotel. The last bomb exploded at the Airport Centaur Hotel at 3:40 PM.

It took only two hours and ten minutes for the people of Mumbai to witness their biggest nightmare ever. As per reports, the blasts left 257 people dead and 713 people were seriously injured while properties worth about Rs 27 crores were destroyed. These blasts had not only attacked the city of Mumbai but also the minds of its citizens. This was the first time they had been exposed to terror at such a massive scale, it had left the people terrified. Many lost their loved ones that day, ordinary people who had left home with a promise to return. The serial blasts left every Mumbaikar's heart aching that day. The entire nation shared was in mourning.

The Mumbai Police now had a major task at hand. It was their responsibility to track down the culprits of the blasts and bring them to justice. The Mumbai police took their investigation to each and every corner of the city with a team of more than 150 personnel under the command of Rakesh Maria, who was in charge of DCP Traffic at the time. The team conducted their investigation meticulously, from the substance used as bombs (RDX) to the intensity of the blasts. No stone was left unturned. During their search, an abandoned scooter and a Maruti van, packed with weapons and hand grenades were discovered. This was the first major lead that propelled the investigation forward.

The police tracked the clues to one name. The van was found to be registered in the name of a Rubina Memon, who was found to be a resident of the Al-Hussainia building in Mahim. The police swiftly paced to the eight-story building where the Memons lived. Upon their arrival, they found that the door was locked. They had no choice but to break in. In an interview in the

Mumbai Mirror[2], Rakesh Maria explained how during the raid, they found a scooter key on the refrigerator. It belonged to the same weapon-loaded scooter they had found earlier. Everything was falling into place. The only hurdle was that the Mumbai Police had arrived at the scene a little too late. The Memons had left India two days before the blasts.

IN HIDING

July 1994
Kathmandu

Yusuf Mohammed Ahmed walked through Tribhuvan International Airport, Kathmandu. He had a Pakistani passport in his hand and had just gotten off his flight from Karachi. He exited the airport to find his cousin Usman, who had arrived to receive him. They took a taxi to Karnoli Hotel, where they had booked a room for themselves. Once they entered the room, it was time for a much-needed conversation between them. Yusuf Mohammed Ahmed was not the man's real identity. He was Yakub Memon, who for the last seventeen months had been living the life of an absconder. He had surrendered mentally and was tired of the life he had been living for the past 17 months.

While there was no information about Tiger Memon, it was revealed later that Yakub and his family had settled down in Dubai. However, this was not to be a happy ending. Shortly after this was revealed to the

[2] https://www.indiatoday.in/india/story/mumbai-blasts-verdict-rakesh-maria-tada-1993-serial-bombings-babri-demolition-abu-salem-983131-2017-06-16

world, they were forced to flee from Dubai. The Indian Government had been pressurising the UAE government to expel the Memons from the country. The Memons were secretly escorted by an ISI agent to Karachi[3], where they were supplied with Pakistani passports and national identity cards. Soon, the Indian Government received information that the Memons were in Karachi. India appealed to the United Nations, the US and various European countries to support their request to Pakistan that the Memons be handed over. Therefore, on 15 April the Memons, escorted by four ISI commandos, took a Thai Airways flight to Bangkok, where they were accommodated in a spacious bungalow on Pattaya Road. They were virtually under house arrest, as they were not allowed to leave the bungalow and were under constant surveillance. After twelve days, the protests by the Memon family grew so intense that they were brought back to Karachi again, where they were housed in the Karachi Development Scheme area, popularly known as Defence Colony and predominantly inhabited by army officials and personnel. This was a high-security zone and meant that the Memons were virtually untraceable: now it was impossible to apprehend them without the cooperation of the Pakistani government. Their lives were, in some sense, better there. But they knew one thing for sure—they would never be truly free again. Yakub was struggling with his past and the choices he had made. He could have remained in Pakistan under the mercy and protection of the government or he could

[3] https://scroll.in/article/744801/the-yakub-memon-story-the-man-who-helped-india-expose-pakistans-role-in-1993-bombay-blasts

go back to India and try to clear his name. This was the reason which made him fly to Kathmandu.

In Kathmandu, Yakub met his lawyer. He had to do something soon. Yakub was thinking about his parents and his wife Raheen, who was due to deliver their child soon. He had a discussion with his lawyer about the options that he had but, unfortunately for him, the situation was not in his favour. He was unlikely to receive any mercy if he surrendered to the Indian authorities. With all hope lost, he prepared to leave for Karachi. Yakub was back at the airport in the morning on 24 July as Yusuf Mohammed Ahmed once again. He had decided to fly back to Karachi. The tables turned against him when he entered the security check. The security officer found two passports belonging to him—Indian and Pakistani—and also, a Pakistani national identity card and a large amount of Pakistani and US currency. News quickly reached the Interpol and later New Delhi. A three-day interrogation began at Kathmandu with both Indian and Nepali police participating in it. Yakub claimed that he had given himself up willingly, the biggest revelation made by him. He and his family were fed up with the continuous monitoring that they faced in Pakistan, which forced him to take this step. He himself provided all the incriminating evidence in his suitcase.

28 July 1994
New Delhi

A blindfolded Yakub was reportedly dropped off at Sunoli, on the border of UP, at 3:00 AM He was hungry and totally drained of energy. From there, he was taken to Gorakhpur, about two hours by road from Sunoli, and then flown to Delhi in a special plane. On the plane, Yakub met Union Home Secretary K Padmanabhaiah who headed the CBI investigation in Delhi. This was the chain of events as described by Yakub when he was presented before the Magistrate. But the CBI continued to claim that he had been arrested at New Delhi Railway Station on 5 August 1994. They had been tipped off about Yakub's location earlier. He was at the station carrying a briefcase. CBI officers, along with armed commandos, were waiting for him. It still remains unclear whether he had surrendered in exchange for a deal to clear his family's name or was it an ambush by the CBI.[4]

After the CBI got their hands on Yakub, he was taken to the CBI headquarters at Lodi Road. The Union Home Minister SB Chavan announced his sensational arrest in the Lok Sabha.

THE INTERVIEW

Yakub had been under CBI custody for twelve days, locked up in a dark cell. The CBI officers interrogated him for hours every day and he answered all their questions. One day, he was informed that he had to appear for an interview which the entire nation would watch. After refusing initially, he later agreed to the interview.

He was taken to the Doordarshan Studio, he was going to be interviewed on Newstrack, a half-hour news analysis show telecasted by the channel. During the interview, he narrated the tale of his journey to Kathmandu, his interception at the airport and being handed over to the CBI.

---

4 https://www.thequint.com/videos/the-gripping-and-uncertain-tale-of-yakub-memons-surrender

He stated that it was Tiger Memon and Taufiq Jaliawala, a Dubai-based ISI agent, who had been the masterminds of the Mumbai blasts. He also revealed the role of Dawood Ibrahim, the notorious Mumbai underworld criminal, and his complicity in the attacks. He used this opportunity to let his countrymen know that apart from Tiger Memon, the other Memons were decent and innocent, that they were law-abiding citizens.

THE CONVICTION

Yakub Memon was kept in Central Prison in Nagpur. The Supreme Court confirmed his participation in financing the Mumbai blasts. His financial acumen made the investigators believe that he had a major role to play in the serial blasts. It was also later confirmed that he was entrusted with the task of handling the explosives and their safekeeping. He was also actively involved in hawala transactions for the purpose of facilitating the blasts. The Supreme Court confirmed Yakub's conviction and death sentence on 21 March 2013 based on the above evidence.

Memon filed a Review Petition for reviewing the Supreme Court's judgment. It did not turn out to be effective. The Supreme Court stood firm on its decision. The bench, headed by Chief Justice P Sathasivam and Justice BS Chauhan, rejected Memon's application on 30 July 2013. Memon's brother Suleman then filed a mercy petition to the president of India on 6 August 2013. But this plea was rejected by President Pranab Mukherjee on 11 April 2014.

By 30 April 2015, the Maharashtra Government was actively working towards finalising the date of execution of Yakub Memon. Post all the official discussions, they confirmed 30 July 2015 as the date for Memon's execution. Memon could see his last day approaching soon. With only three months ahead of him, he filed a curative petition before the Supreme Court on 22 May 2015. He hoped for a favourable response this time, a chance to escape the death sentence. Yet again, his hopes were crushed, the curative petition was rejected on 21 July 2015.

With no other option left in front of him, Memon filed a mercy petition addressed to the governor of Maharashtra. His petition claimed that the death warrant issued against him was illegal. Simultaneously, he also filed a writ before the Supreme Court of India for a stay on his execution till the mercy petition was reviewed. In midst of all the filing and rejection of petitions, he continued his dedication towards education. While in prison, he earned two Master's degrees. He earned his first Master's degree in English literature in 2013 and the second degree in 2014 in political science.

THE FINAL ACT

On the eve of his execution, Yakub Memon was sleeping, perhaps not a peaceful sleep, until he was woken up at 4:00 AM. He was then asked to take a warm bath and a fresh set of clothing was provided to him. He expressed his wish to read the holy book before he met his death. After reading the Quran and doing *salah*, he was given the last meal of his choice. He had one more wish, his last wish—to talk to his daughter, one last time before the noose tightened around his neck. Before he breathed his last, he was allowed to speak to his daughter. The only thing that remained was the medical examination.

Yakub Memon was hanged around 6:30 AM on 30 July 2015, on his 53rd birthday in Nagpur Central Prison.

Acknowledgements

I would like to thank a few people without whose constant support this book would not have been possible. God—I owe this book to you as you gave me the courage to write on such a huge idea. Dad, who always inspired me to complete anything that I have started, and Mom, whose love and care plodded me to achieve more, my wife Neha Jain and my son Granth Deep Jain.

Thanks to my siblings, Deepika Jain and Deepali Jain, and my brother-in-law Nikhil Jain. Their love, constant teasing and feedback motivated me to keep writing.

A special thanks to Shreejit Nair, who despite the busy man he is, still managed to go through the manuscript and offered his valuable suggestions.

I cannot forget to thank my best buddy and partner at Happee Chips Foundation, Taran Singh Thakur, who is always there when I need a friend.

Last, but not the least, I thank Shreya Chakraborti, Editorial Manager, and Paul Vinay Kumar, Publisher, Special Projects, Bloomsbury Publishing India and the entire Bloomsbury team who led this project to its fruition.

Acknowledgements

About the Author

Prateek Jain is an advocate and a senior advisor to Innovis Law Partners, a law firm based in Bhopal. His expertise lies in civil and criminal law. He is also the co-founder of a snacks manufacturing company called Happee Chips. The president of a non-profit organisation called the Granth Education Society, Bhopal, Prateek has also been a visiting faculty of Vision Infinity, Bhopal—one of the premiere IIT JEE coaching institutes in central India. Prior to that, he was the director of IMS Bhopal and the Universal Institute of Legal Studies (UILS), Bhopal, a popular CLAT (Common Law Admission Test) preparation institute.

Passionate about teaching, Prateek started his career as the director of a coaching centre called Achievers' Bank. He joined UILS (Universal Institute of Legal Studies) as an academic coordinator and headed the Department of Analytical Reasoning there. Later, he worked as a Senior Knowledge Executive in LAWRYTHYMS at C-Lead, Bhopal.

While pursuing a teaching career, Prateek has also realized his writing aspirations. He has authored two educational books—*Logical Reasoning* (2011) and *Elementary Mathematics* (2012). Following which, he also published two fiction titles—*Eleven Rhythms of Life* (2013) and *Dream in the Secret* (2014).